HAPPINESS BASTARD

ALSO BY KIRBY DOYLE

Sapphobones (Poets Press, 1966)

Ode to John Garfield (Communiciation Company, 1967)

Angel Faint (Communication Company, 1968; Deep Forest, 1991)

The Collected Poems of Kirby Doyle (Greenlight Press, 1983)

After Olson (Deep Forest, 1984)

The Questlock Gymnopaean of A. Dianaei O'Tamal (Deep Forest, 1987)

Lyric Poems (City Lights, 1988)

Crime, Justice & Tragedy and Das Erde Profundus (Deep Forest, 1989)

Pre American Ode (unpublished)

White Flesh (unpublished)

HAPPINESS BASTARD
KIRBY DOYLE

TOUGH POETS PRESS
ARLINGTON, MASSACHUSETTS

Front cover photo courtesy of the estate of Kirby Doyle.

Back cover photo by Chuck Gould, San Francisco, 1968.

ISBN 978-0-578-73203-9

This edition published in 2020 with permission
from the estate of Kirby Doyle by
Tough Poets Press
Arlington, Massachusetts 02476
U.S.A.

www.toughpoets.com

1.

What time spaced the arrows of Misfortune's Buttercup?

There is much in the palindrome of Signes, Clockes & Fires, but not yon Light what gathers on ye Eye . . .

It is the glare . . .

THE GLARE!

A junkie's vein knows more angry majik from the foul-fingered grave than all the pretty barks of Poetry . . .

yea! so be it Established, Crank'd or Song'd: Write Precious & suck Agony, O thou Tasty Tortures of Time!

Radix 1: Apologia Poetica. Laboured upon yon vague hill (trees twisted truncate & twigs & tight sky motted w'th'drippings of dawn) iron newsreels jerking, Singless Voices of Unribboned Glory (crack'd idiom's delight!)

spin out the imprecise Zodiacs of the City.

The City Insidious . . . croaking with teachers & mothers, spiked the Voice like a captured cannon . . . hobbled bulls the boys brilliant with the Ax of Song . . . tedious maxims of the mind awash & extending through tepid years (the sound-box weakened!), the rules kept tight by the constant contractions of the Liberal Sphincter, the professorial passing of wind, perhaps even the ever-planned leakage of turdy moisture rivering down among the cracks of the rostrum, over the Old Duff's Shoes, across the gizzards of untenured fellows (. . . leaking in the President's breakfast!) . . . all this pick & drop of innards of tooth nerves nails & veins . . . all the baited watchment for the rips & rattles of faint unfused pre-flashed passions for gotten under the sly lubrication of false outer oils . . . yea, Treacherous Welcome . . . hidey-holes yawning open into which as the threatened thought scuttles from sentence to sentence it be ready to scramble at the slightest Stench & Gesture of that glare-eyed Syntax up & down upon which so many of my Brethren in these ruptured times wolde do march their sexheads off to what undiscovered wars . . . timorous undulations of Safety cuddling the brain ("Ile haue me braines tane out & Butter'd & giue them to a dog for a newe yeare's gifte!") critically (solemn noddingly dedicated to the Educatement of Youths . . .) mime-ing flabourous fields of sea-anemone/crystalline whiskers of sensibility sucked back upon contact with unedible notions & such . . . cellophaned taste packed in proto-jelly . . . hankies of morality/semantic membranes clinging to the Face & Sight . . . infernal fingers ripe w'the gore of dissected wit . . . & . . . ORGANIZED CRIME . . . !

Slippery inventions ooze through the Learned Fingers (The Eucharist pre-formulated and set to Icy Periods of Art) manipulating the Clutches & Levers of Historie . . . ahh, the Vague Dears crouched among the spears of doubt like aged virgins hoping for one unlettered truth to seduce their fear.

Yet even Doubt (". . . more cruel than the worst of truths . . ." —this . . . habited hysteria reaching for the Eyes) can smell of sour poverty . . . the fungus of fear proposes Immediate Treatment . . . the wandering scholar is signaled warning and floating messages appear: "Understatement-Is-The-Emphasis-Of-The-Civilized," from the bland & Cultured Critic . . . and then (of course) p . . . y as ". . . the spontaneous overflow of powerful feelings recollected in tranquility" from (of course) The Powerfully Tranquille Recollections of a Spontaneously Successful Poet . . . & Etcetera ad infinitum safely guided down through the mediumistic communication of endless doctorial dissertations.

The interchangeable ballistics of human love fade in scholastic tears like a child's wash-drawing left to the rain.

Ancient discourses can do no more than wait to be read again & conjure the aged hateful image:

STROKE THE GANGLION!!!!

(I show my teeth . . .)

So it is here that I gather myself with reasonably empty bowels to fashion a 30 foot hand-written Historie Of All Things Past. It has been asked, "How come them too?"

Now, where do we begin? Yes, how do we begin? (DO WE BEGIN?)

Be gentle, O Funny Fornicators
& put aside lewd snickers . . .

2.

BIRTH, SALVATION & EXCITED ADDENDA

O Pre-Lubricated Dawn of the City, I Jason (Prince?) come to suck the cold brown almond heart of a gull from among the sealice and feathered shell . . . yea, and here will I hug my awkward poems like Cleo's angry asp . . .

(uncareful bandages shift)

(". . . and here the onion skin cap of fear eat fear yaaaah sitting tight on the moist righteous head slips down over one ear and remarks upon itself by all means put yerself together and remove it from the vision, so doing same and viewing same and being same I calmly left the wholewe phucking shtt/n mtch.

yrs truly, nfh"

this,
expansively introjected upon my writing machine by an
aging blond paintrix possessed of a plentiful and corpu-
lent bum about whose left eyes entwines a most bounteous mouse, there affixed by the judicious fist of The
Rat Bastard & Who, when Hunger Struck and I repaired
swiftly through the nightly gloom & murk to the Universal Cafe (which is next to a huge cube, grayish-brown in
color, owned by one Tao Lee Yon and some good distance
from the Bemus Bag Co. where at one time labored The
Leonic Ogre amongst the sweltering vats of fat rubber for
molds & such, not to mention the A& W Root Beer Bar),
was drunkenly propped against my kitchen wall and was
gone when I returned.)

"So too do I single combat upon the Molecular Whales
of Knowledge who pronounce conditions upon the gov-
ernment of Mind with attendant curses upon "wayward
and faithless" Visions & Imaginings!! . . . !!"

I cannot cry . . . (the theme for today?)

. . . .

The Old Endless Seed:

I was to tell you of certain tribulations in The Making
of Art, but . . . when The Man Inside becomes The Man
Outside the Point of View (locus, focus, her magic tokas)
shifts:

"Use a bone buttone in yer pot-pipe; only 4 easy holes to clean."

Samuel Taylor Cool

I shall begin this Historie, or rather the Narrative Portion thereof (note the numerous crescendos), mainly because to my quainted way of thinking (tho perhaps not endings; i.e., Aladdin Ginstrap re: Nuncle Billy Burroughs) are unshirkable (note: responsibility, the cause of a clabbered spleen), yes and will thus begin with an hour of Erotica, during said hr, whilst clapped in the chilly grasp of Methamphetamine, I observed me giving myself head. I do begin thus not only to arouse those passions generally provoked by clinical pornography but also to give my vague reader some indication of the state in which my meth-soaked & cannabis cuddled brain is not at rest. This is to say that some nights ago I found myself abed with my Little Bisquit, both of us being in a rubbing state of arousement. As is my wont, I fetched my tongue & fingers over, around and into the more erotic pieces of her body (22 yrs, 5 ft. & 3 ins., 106 lbs., unsagged but soft handful breasts, evening-blue eyes & lids encircled with Egyptian black painted lines, henna-rusted hair bursting from her head to entwine her nipples) and as my 3 day bristle of unshaven chin began to comb the fine-curled and pale tops of her pubic hair my mind, throwing sparkling light-years of sex past my eyes, arced out like a cosmic yo-yo and gave me her perspective on the proceedings: from her eyes I watched and felt the Tongued Sex of my own cunticular ("In his cun()icular day." —Anecdote of Lodwick Muggleton (1676), (Davies) . . .) activities; that is, her Sight became mine while my Body remained my own, and I not only saw, felt and understood the giving, but also Saw, Felt & Understood the Receiving. And so she to me head still from her eyes & her sight My Watching from behind Her Eye Orbs as her-my mouth took in my organ and or my tongue & lips against the moist-folded vanilla sweetness (the Leonic Ogre suggested this flavor and I concur only out of a panicked descriptive ineptitude) of hers-mine! I would allow this fitting of my View over her Brain much analagous to the tightening of a wet leather glove clinging to the hand but not controlling it, rather is controlled by it the hand still but inside a complete shift of Tactile Dimension. Do you follow? It not only feels different but almost stuns (Reason Gone) my transvested genital windows. Irving asked of me once, "Have you ever sucked a cock?" (this while urging me away from a timidity of purpose "within the poem" . . . Paul C. wrote too, "I don't find you cutting *into* the poem . . .") and I owned that I had not, limiting as I had my queer flutterings to faint smiles and coy clasps; just once allowing, and this at 16 and as a soldier-boy of the Republic's army, a lonely (he said) buddy to jack me off in a scrub-oak forest, but not finding the instant pressure of

12

brain on muscle needed to reach over and grab his joint.
What shall I answer now?

Pierre, it will be remembered, ". . . madly demanded
more ardent Fires . . ." but I . . . ? . . .

Ah . . . were I only a queer contortionist!

. . . .

"Ben Johnson had one eie lower than t'other, and
bigger, like Clun the player. Perhaps he begott Clun."

John Aubrey

. . . .

Radix 2: Primum Mobile.

What this purpose Life? Why, most sweetened sire, to
travel thru the Planet! To move about upon this blitzed
and blistered round of dank and mildewed matter . . . to
let the Feather fly! In the words of the Leonic Ogre (upon
whom I lean so heavy the imprints of my elbows are per-
manent upon his brow) "You can't fix it and you can't
make it go away." We seem to be stuck with the bugger . . .
clumsy sphere tugging us in vacant directions.

Haroo, haroo! Whither goes the goose? Look at it, this
eggy ball of dirt wandering through the universe in ellip-
tical spasms . . . O look and see what unpretty actions we
commit upon it, poor lumpy thing . . . dig howling holes

deep and painful into it, gouge ragged trenches across its skin, tear and bite the leafy growths from its offering grasp, construct sharp and ugly objects atop it, shower poisons down upon it, clutter it with the decomposition of weary bodies, rusty philosophies and the rubbled leakage of human life, then rage wars and agonies of disputations demand for possession of it, and then once possessed . . . despised . . . smashed and sundered for its fuels and motions . . . never once touching thought as we strain to weaken this mute and voiceless orb that with all our brained hypotheses of time, space & speed we have no better vehicle with which to tour the infinite universe than the battered globe beneath our feet. I should not wonder if it were as anxious to be rid of us as are we to flee its gentle limitations.

Listen . . .

Can you feel the weight of this earth revolving beneath us, its grams & pounds & ounces spinning after Stars & Suns & Spaces?

3.

Tully McSwine Stalks The Planet:

Had an applesauce sandwich for breakfast and a glass
of wine too; great, cheap, vinegary wino-type wine that
when you puke comes bubbl'n out yer nose and stings
a bit. Had another glass after breakfast and feel a whole
hell of a lot better for it too. Can hear the clucks of dis-
approval from dry hearts the land over came rattl'n down
me flue, but I don't give one screaming good goddamn.
Give me the fuzzy feeling anytime and ye baggy crones
and hags can go boil yer heads in great steaming tubs of
Baptist spittle. Cluck till yer iron tongues tear loose and
rusty from yer chalky skulls! Hiss away, great toadies of
contentment, and preach withered sermons of sobriety
whilst I prance merry in my glass-handled grave! When
flat-ass purity is the only vice within my means I'll fart in
the coin box and whistle Jingle Bells in hell!

Drink holds no sorrows. Too much misunderstanding

about that little point. I can hear lurky clouds of steam rumbling in my bowels and clabbered vapors fill my head. I stagger . . . I reel . . . I fall to the booger-filthy mattress and the curdled miseries of my guts. Has the Drunkards Doom come rattling out of the hidey-holes of Eternity eons before my time? Eh? What's that? Do I hear the scuffle of humankind barking outside my hidden windows? Life Lives! The Globe whirls on! Saved again . . . must be my lucky year. I'll find me a hunchback and rub his hump . . . that should keep a good thing going.

I have a second glass of Old Rot-Yer-Guts and contemplate the blackened tips of my toes. To wash or not to wash? That isn't a question. Whether it would be nobler in my pose to suffer a bit of self-abuse . . . a swift whack at the private parts . . . or to bathe the lower extremities? The former has been known to drive a body snot-run'n-out-yer-nose mad . . . no need to push a good thing too far. Ah me now, the toes it is then, and a goodly wash under the armpits and down the backside might not be too damaging to the person. Up we go then! Ugh . . . easy there, sailor! Leave out a little slack! Some low-life oaf is stomping about in my upper stories. Hey you! Leave off! Soft you now. There. That's better. O look at me. A frigging mess. Who's been boiling garbage on my tongue? Must have been baking mud cakes last night . . . eating them too. Zap! Don't touch me with those fingers! Can't help it, Sport, they belong to you. Easy then . . . with the tips.

What a crusted raggedy-ass bastard I am! I'll need a chisel
to chip the crud.

Up off me arse. Down me hole with what is left of this
evil brew. Scratch me fanny. Up me nose-hole to the first
joint of me little finger. Something there, by Gaud! Snag
it under the nail. It's stringy with a bit of blood on the
anchoring end. Gaaa! Out into the hall to the can. For the
love of God . . . don't go barefooted! Feet'll rot off at the
ankles. Couldn't stand that. Large pencil scrawl on the
wall over the john:

> PLEASE DO NOT THROW BUTTS IN THE
> CRAPPER AS THIS MAKES THEM WET AND
> SOGGY AND HARD TO LIGHT.
> THANK YOU.

Shows talent.

Back into my room. Slam the door as hard as I can. A
Puerto Rican curse comes filtering down the hall at me.
"Up yer bum!" I shout back. Over the sink. One lousy tap.
Cold water. Cheap bastards. String up all the landlords
one of these days. Hang 'em by the flusher chains with
their feet dangling in the festering toilet bowls. Punish
my hands and face in the icy water. Hike up one foot, then
the other. Don't get carried away with it, though. That'll
do. A quick swab under the arms and across the belly. I
shudder to my soul. Wobble over to the mattress and flop.

On with the socks (rank) and shoes (stolen). Scab around in the busted coffee cup and dig out a butt long enough to poison myself with. Struggle into my Goodwill clothes. Stand up. Sway a bit. Make a grab at the walls of my rotting room. Wish I had a small lacer of sweet wine to put me right. All gone though. I sigh like a backsliding stoic. I glance out the wrinkled window. Sun's gonna be bright. Look around for my trusty shades. Find them in my breast pocket. One lens cracked and one ear-hook slightly taped with a nasty piece of adhesive. Wind my electric-yellow scarf around my handsome neck. Must look like an old-time movie tycoon gone to blast. Ah well, I'm ready . . . out I go into this old world with the measurements of a new day.

*　　*　　*

Onto the street. Lower East Side decaying like God's Great Gloomy Splendor. East 2nd Street in the gray dusty afternoon. Have to squint against the flying filth. The street looks like a still gray snake with rag and newspaper parasites fluttering down its spine. Cold! Damn me! Chill fingers shatter my earlobes like bitter balls of ice. I hug my old jacket against the razor wind. Old belt-in-the-back tweed sports job circa 1927. Very stylish. Too bad fashions fade.

Everybody head down, neck in, watch-the-hell-out-for-yerself. I go to cross Avenue A and a fleshy cabbie screams a hysterical curse at me . . . almost rams truck and screams at truckdriver . . . truckdriver screams back . . . cop walks over screaming . . . mass hysteria begins to catch hold as cop . . . cabbie . . . truckdriver and two howling women pedestrians all break down screaming with much waving of arms. I am delighted. The globe spins on. I let out three horrible whoops and dash across the street. Nobody on the street pays the slightest attention to the madness going on at the intersection. Normal intercourse of daily living. I am just a wholesome youth going about my father's business.

I trot on the street to keep my cold guts from solidifying. Late afternoon. The sun slides in the sky. Look! There! Squinting through slits between the suffering buildings . . . the sky crisp as chips and blue as meadows. Walking south. The day hangs exhausted. Down Avenue A to Houston Street. Great torn-up cinders-in-yer-eye type street. Up Houston bordered by ever-waiting vacant lots . . . hard, desolate, wasted ground tangled by piles of broken bricks, burnt black mounds of ash, dirty bushes. Tenements . . . five, seven stories high backed up to the edge of the wasted land. Sad strings of dying wash hung high up from window to window. Every now and again a cold mourner squints across the rooftops from behind a sooty window pane. Delicate birds balance on the ledges. Ferocious gangs of paste-colored children scream along the edge of buildings. A ruined cat crawls belly-flat to the ground. The sun is there but so thin, so far away. I turn off Houston into Orchard Street. Insane pushcart-crowded street! The sidewalks dangerous from gesturing hands flying about my face in a frenzy of barter. Floppy men and women with worn and dusty eyelids chant at the beginnings of my curiosity then turn to sneery gossip again as I move away to other views of their hectic wares. I wander along among the clutching hands that snap out to grab at my sleeve like a forest of dull knives trembling to slash me limbless. Smiling mouths beckon to me from lurky doorways. My mouth smiles back. Like some old plagued and rotty world this street crumbles in upon itself. Old and antique Jews in big round black hats, black coats that almost sweep the street, black and graying Jehovah-type beards down to the belly button, stringy side-curls writhing about their ears. Yes yes O Lord! Stalls, stalls, stalls, and women with bundles haggling, begging . . . some rocklike, firm, unbending, take so much nonsense, no more . . . some crushed under by stall-keeper scorn. Food stalls, clothing, yardage, knives, toys, bread, beds. The language . . . the din bobs in my ears . . . twisted inversions of two, three tongues.

I move on. An old creature in a cloth cap comes scuttling at me sideways from the stale hole of a doorway, hooks his greasy fingers into my cuff and comes near to jerking me smash onto my head. Panic stomps on my liver. My kidneys quake. A thin trickle of pee warms my thigh. Is he a sex fiend? A near-sighted rapist? A cut-purse? The Mad Bomber?

"You wanna buy? I got it! Best buys!" His words slither over me like a drunkard's breath. I want to turn away but am afraid to. I smile like a coward and unhook myself from his claws. He violently waves me toward his stall and I move awkwardly toward it . . . wanting to flee but afraid again . . . afraid he might call scorn and abuse after me . . . afraid I would have to hurry past a streetful of stall-keepers with humiliation leaking from my head. I stop and look.

A sidewalk shop full of plaster statues of a holy sort. Little clumsy Christs by the dozen, molded Marys, athletic apostles and a score of plaques with bleeding hearts bursting with evangelical gore. Christian statuary by the gross lot. Crucifixions line the stall . . . reproductions of that happy butchery to tack above the bed . . . The Castigated Carpenter bleeding down the wall, over the shoes, along the floor, under the door and into the streets . . . inundating all the Christian lands with the righteous power of blood and chastity while we sleep tight under this sorrow.

"What'a ya want? Jeezus maybe?" His lizard hands crawl among the statues. He stares at me. One side of his face curls in an expectant sneer, the other half frozen, his pebbly eyes considering price, profit. The hideous play slips inside me. I feel weak. I giggle and sag a bit. I giggle again and try to stop, but the grotesque invites me with a gracious wave and my giggle becomes a mean and slimy laughter slapping him back and forth across the teeth. He looks at me as if half my head had slipped off. Then he begins to regurgitate a polluted little snicker of defense at my derangement.

I was roaring, almost shouting my laughter. Folks began to stare. My scabby old shopkeeper in the cloth cap began to blink nervously . . . his asshole eyes clanking open and shut as if some crippled gnome were inside his head turning a handle. His face looked like an atrophied doll's head that you could tilt back and forth to open and shut the stiff lids. My laughter echoed in his stall as if in a moonish crater. He looked as though he were about to swoon. *Did I Want A Jesus Christ?* It was a question to ponder.

Yes, by my Mammy's tattered hopes, I did, and a whole heap of salvation too. Want to soak in the Blood of the Lamb? My path is strewn with the broken hearts of family and friends. Want redemption from the bright evils that lurk in me eyes? Wildness fondles my damnation! Ah, the self-abuse that's in me! I smile at him. He teeters in his skin.

"Got one that glows in the dark?" Want to have the godly example shining a'fore my eyes whether it come night or day, sleeping or awake, in sickness or in health, till death do me apart and I slip down the greased slide to hell or other regions of Christian imagination.

"You betcha!" Fumbles around in back like an old pervert after a schoolboy's fly. Comes up with one that looks like all the rest.

"How do I know that it glows in the dark?"

"Here, I show you." Beckons me into coffin-sized hole of a shop behind the stall. Dinky little forty-watt bulb weakly burning amid the boxed Saviours. Flicks off the bulb. Spooky. Dark as a well-digger's ass. Holds up Jesus. By Gaud He glows! His crude little stamped-out face throwing out a murky halo. I'm delighted! Here, let me hold it. A genuine assembly-line miracle. Bet if I kiss it it'll shed a tear. I do. It does. Or is it just one of mine?

"Ya like'ut?" He leers at me. "A dolla item. Letcha have'ut fa six bits."

Money is no consideration. Couldn't stand to haggle over a religious article. A real honest-to-goodness-manufactured-in-Indiana icon. Must have it. None o'yer pigs bones for me. I dig in my pocket for money. Not much there but I hand him his due. Into my coat pocket goes our Saviour. If threatened I just outs with our Lord and waves Him at the vampire who goes slinking and hissing and cringing back till he melts into a pool of mung. Feel safer now.

*   *   *

All the emotion had set a dryness to scrambling about in my throat. A little drop needed to soothe an unseasonable mid-winter drought. Drink's a comfort. There's biblical authority for that. Look at Noah. Great sailor. God knows the faithful . . . can set yer watch by that. Let it come down, O Lord! I'm yer man.

Spot a large peely sign, *Pal's Rendezvous*. Zip, I goes into the cozy tavern. Place smells of sick cheer. Ah, the sight of it. The Homeless huddled over good nickle glasses of sweet cheer. Puts flame to the innards. Keeps the dew from the daisy. I ups to the bar. Foot on the rail. A large piece of fuzzy meat that finally focuses into a jowly barkeep with three days worth of beard leans over to me. Smile, stranger.

"What's yours?"

"Ten cents worth o' th' drip'ns from yer daddy's hatband, Henry."

"Muscatel?"

"Yer privy to me very thoughts."

He sets up a water glass the size of a jam jar and fills it brim shivering full with the golden juice. I stares at it for a moment to let the foreign matter settle a bit, then picks it up and quaffs it down. Tears explode from my leaky eyes . . . a 160-foot square-rigger name of the John Good built by Bathscope & Sons in Boston in 1873 slides down the ways into my lower intestine. A good vintage. I drop a dime onto the bar and it disappears under the barkeep's fat palm. That's what we needed. A little depth charge. Blow the fish from the sea. Cleans the seaweed from the entrails. I order another.

Bare lightbulbs hung by twisted cords down the length of the room, a scarred bar along one side, beaten booths along the other with a few wobbly tables in the back. Just a joint for the tattered hungry to wander in and squander their few loose pennies on the sweet giggly joyous juice. It was steamy warm and radiated a stale camaraderie among the ragged drinkers. I felt at home. I glowed a bit. I sipped. Time vanished like a frightened child.

I watched a scene . . . a play without passion. In the corner booth four battered men sat and rolled and flung their arms around each other in fitful familiarity. Scabs from stumbling in doorways were pasted over their faces. The garments that covered their bodies seemed hidey-holes for crawly creatures. Fingers twitched, eyes crumbled, tongues licked limply in search of lips. Noses were raw reservoirs for a constant stream of snot to wipe across grimy fingers and knuckles between snuffles. Long, tangled, greasy twists of hair hung onto their faces. Little balls of dust collected dried mucus and spittle and the slobberings of drink and food clung in the untouchable whiskers. The sounds coming from the yellowed mouths had a wavering diseased tremor. An almost invisible vapor of decay hung over their party. I watched them, the minutes rotting by.

They babbled and patted each other and sang and swore and gagged and hocked up evil-looking lungers to be dropped on the floor, and I watched. I sipped my poison and put my head on the bar and stared close at the grainy wood. I saw my tears. The wood smelled of sour poverty. I licked the bar with the tip of my tongue and tasted the fungus of fear. The interchangeable ballistics of human love faded in my tears like a child's wash-drawing left to the rain. I heard the rips of passion unroll parchment-like beneath my skin. I think I slept.

My eyes opened after some part of time had crumbled. The withered men still sat in their tatters. The barkeep was asleep at the end of the bar. The place was otherwise empty. One of the trembling dipsos raised up to his feet and held out his glass.

"To my Mother," he gasped and dumped the booze down his hole. The others clapped and made gurgling noises of approval and drooled into their hooch and spat and slapped their toasting companion in congratulations at his successful conjuring of an ancient hateful image. Rage leaked from my eyes and dripped into my lap. Obscenities and vile oaths hollered empty in my head . . . but I'm a blue-eyed chap and curly haired so I just showed my teeth and hissed.

* * *

Outside . . . the street . . . the city . . . the darkness! O how the night was with me, taunting the rolls of thought that cuddled my brain. My memory like an old piano roll . . . four hot hands at the keys . . . wobbly fingers in my mind . . . my whole life ragtime in broken shoes . . . tiny mallets striking the strings of my soul . . . Ah, Tim, I tell you there's a tune left in the old box yet.

Twenty-seven echoing years pumped by the legs of time . . . invisible fingers make my music . . . such flash'n of hands and arms was never meant to be seen by the likes of me . . . drives the poor poets to frenzy . . . can't put words to the clatter in my skin . . . like old bones dancing in an aching hall.

I stood in the midnight of my mind and could sense The Man In The Bright Nightgown lurking about in the memory of my years . . . Kid Sorrow turned his back and huddled against the chill wind that swept from my ruptured lust . . . Mad Jack rattled broken bottles, kicked a rotting window, then shrieking like an unpaid whore he scaled a board fence and disappeared down the dusty back alley of my fear.

. . . .

Item No. 3: I'm looking at the world through snot-colored glasses.

4.

McSwine Strikes A Classic Pose:

Must I obey my grief? I kick a cowardly copy of Time's anonymous cynicism (very second-rate cynicism . . . more like a prose gargle) out of me way up against a lamppost where the puppie-dogs could make do with it and hustled my chilly earlobes down the street toward Cooper Union hoping to be in time for the last complete show (The Ghost of Lincoln Stalks the Boards: ". . . fuck you Sandburg, bone-picker of my quiet memory . . . leave my frightened wife and tad for me to wrap in my own bony arms").

God's Glorious Guts! The night was black! I stood in the midnight of my mind, the blackout of my existence! I could hear the wardens of morality rattling at my doors, "Turn off them Eyes there! Turn off them Eyes I say or we'll shoot 'em out!" I blinked me lids and held out me claw. "PENNIES FOR A POOR BLIND BASTARD!" but no one answered except a decaying juice-head sitting on an ashcan and snuffling against the chilly winds that blow and shake the anchors of the world . . . rattling the murky chains a'tween decks. "Have a drink, buddie," he sez to me holding out a loathsome fifth. "Have a drink and ferget yer troubles. The World, the Night, the Street ain't what she used to be when Ole' Lonesome was running things. The Soul Discontent cain't hardly find a night's flop no'ers. Have a drink!"

I do and thanks to ye, I nodded.

"Drink up and hate the world ya live in . . . Black the Tongue & Red the Eye! . . . hate the world ya live in! Drink up I say!"

I do again and fight down the puke that geysers in my guts.

"Rely on drink and ferget the Human Heart . . . the old Pump's been buggered by Belief . . . swill away, ho ho, swill away . . . Faith Corrupts! . . . pour it down me son, pour it down!"

I kill the jug and he cracks the neck from another . . . jagged gapes the neckless bottle that I raise to my lips.

"Beware the pus-eyed sky-pilot in a bed-sheet shout'n us down the Glory Road! Rinse yer gums me son and let it leak!"

I lower the bottle to find that I've slashed my lips and they've fallen back into my mouth. I spit them out on the pavement and take another pull at the jug.

"Believe me, Tim, the human body is a humble bag of maggot meat . . . cain't lift yer hat from yer head without finding some Salvation Army breathing there!"

My lips begin whispering to me from the sidewalk and I kick them off behind the ash can so's I wouldn't have to listen to them.

"Hope's a gastric rumble in yer guts . . . murder on all fronts . . . charity's an old pair of shoes mouldering among the used bones of a goodwill hype shop."

I nod distracted and begin to worry about my lips.

"If I had my way and Ole' Lonesome was alive, why then . . . why then . . . why then . . . why then . . . why then . . . why then . . ."

He was stuck so I reached over and punched him up-side the head.

". . . why then, by God's Body, things 'ud be different! Ha ha! Why, shiiit ! Look at the way things is be'n run . . . the President's wife gets buggered on her birthday and uses Faith for a douche . . . it all adds up . . . the Universe is a Celestial Misformation spawned by a clapped-up Cupid in a Cosmic Cathouse . . . History, a self-intoxi-cated jack-off; a Gory Essay on festered pages smirking at the unspeakable brutalities heroes of one elevation or the other have committed for the love of something as equally vacuous as heroism . . . don't listen to them, boy . . . Watch & Wait . . . Ole' Lonesome is a'coming back and *He'll* root 'em out!"

"Who?" sez I.

"Who what?" sez he.

"Root *who* out?" I replies.

"Who? Who? Why I'll tell you *who!* Hygienic Nests of Deceivers, that's who! . . . hiding lawfully born citizens from the eyes of Authority! . . . fathers dripping with footballs and sex manuals shown a regulation-sized rubber baby with interchangeable sex . . . mothers told they issued forth nothing but a Blast of Air . . . Congress kept in the dark . . . confused by silence . . . The Hearst Press uncertain . . . who? . . . WHO? . . . by God I'll tell you who! . . . Chiang Kai-shek, that's who! . . . I'm not afraid to speak out and say WHO WHO WHO WHO! The Yellow Peril setting out in the wrong direction and invading Mexico . . . that's who! . . . a Balloon Disaster over the Nation's Capital spilling Oil & Blood down over a well-known (but unnamed) National Monument while the Senate scurries about fumbling at its Collective Fly! . . . a coast-to-coast TV hookup of Billy The Kid jacking-off the ghost of Buffalo Bill! . . . ha ha, that's who! . . . a Saturday Evening Post cover springing to action and chasing Time right up Life's ass! . . . and you have the pecker to ask me who . . . there are ten thousand *whos* . . . the spirit of Silent Cal haunting the White House in search of his lost galoshes . . . Hoover's reusable chicken-in-every-pot flapping in the Arlington National Cemetery . . . The Unknown Soldier evicted from his grave! . . .

look up! WHO leaking from the sky! . . . look down! . . . WHO sprouting from cow-slips! . . . don't ask me *who!* . . . the Eskimo Ambassador wiping his ass on the Confederate Flag! . . . that's who! . . . Good God Jesus Jimmy, look around you! . . . the Pope taking a leak from the left eye of The Statue of Liberty! . . . Deceased members of the DAR copulating with statues of The Southern Dead on the White House lawn . . . Bullmoose eating Tippecanoe in the Holy Waters of the Potomac . . . the ten oldest members of the French Academy raping an Action Group of the WCTU . . . the Vice President farting in the sandbox of history . . . the Spanish Pretender snapping at the bubbles in the bathtub! . . . 70 million Indian Untouchables drowning in a spontaneous flood of semen . . . ! . . . ! . . . ! . . . the whole world standing in a sea of shit up to its chin murmuring, '. . . don't make waves . . . don't make waves . . . don't make waves . . . !' . . . and you ask me WHO? . . . all . . . all this Thread of Chaos woven into the tapestry of Destruction only because Mankind totters about on the rotting limbs of BELIEF!!!! Here, Tim, have a snort of the jug and read this," he sez, handing me the bottle and a Flame-Red Tract with Big Black Letters. I take a shot of the juice and read the handbill:

NO PORK HAM FAT BLOOD EATERS SAVED!
(fried steak full of blood . . .)
STALKING BEASTS IS ABOMINATION . . .

. . . ANTI-JESUS STATES & NATIONS
ARISE
&
HEED
RAVENING WOLVES & IMAGES!
FALSE PLUMAGE OF THE BIRDS OF PROPHET
& SATAN'S POWER PLUS
DEVIL CRUELTY IN THE CLOUDS!
FOR THIS END TIME SPIRIT BREAD &
LIFE MONEY MINUS PROPERTY SOON . . . !!!
IMAGE HATRED & NOISOME SORE . . . MARK!
GESTURE JESUS SHAKING SOON . . . !!!
JESUS SAVED HIS WRATH & DEALS HIS PEOPLE
WHEN HE SOON COMES!
(TESTIMONIES OF UNREPENTANT
MINISTERS * * *)
SET WORTHLESS WATCH FOR IT . . .
THE END SHALL NOT COME!! !! !!

I looked around for my lips but couldn't find them; instead, there behind the ash can squatted my Mind . . . gray archways . . . a million windows . . . all the venerable wreckage of a Feudal Keep. Shifting my gaze I saw that he had stepped on my lips and was hiding them from my sight. "You're stepping on my lips," I said quietly. He didn't move, only sneer'd a little snake smile at me, so I whipped a blade out of my fly and chopped his foot off three inches above the ankle. "That'll teach you," I said, wiping the gutter grime off my lips and fitting them back into my mouth. "The End Shall Not Come . . . ," he hissed at me.

"How come you know so goddamn much!" I shouted through lips rusting from my tears. He raised one reptilian claw in the air and waved a tarnished and tubercular crucifixion and screamed:

"BEWARE, SONNY . . . DON'T DIE THE DEATH YER DADDY DID!" and then tumbled and disappeared down into the bowels of the ash can from which he preached.

My own bowels loosen and sag a bit . . . I reach down and cinch up the draw-string on my sphincter and feel safer. Do I take too much upon myself? Claim a significance that is not mine? O O O, if only Christ had bled less . . . wait! . . . I see . . . a vision vaguely . . . a small yellow daisy growing alone in the center of a vast and desolate land . . . now I see a lean woman slowly walking to it from across the barrenness . . . the skin on her skull is sucked into the hollow shape . . . a face she has used many times . . . she stops . . . she looks down on the flower and hoists her ragged and filthy dress . . . she drops her undergarments fetid and caked . . . she squats over the flower and looks away across the naked wastes . . . she smiles . . . she thinks nothing . . .

*　*　*

O Hart! Hart! Are there cruel bottoms to the sea?

5.

McSwine Piddles The Human Condition:

Move through the city. I standing dread and waterless saluting (as I was . . .) the counterfeit Arch de Triumphe having just (as I had done . . .) relieved myself into the shallow slime of the kiddies pool (lurky monsters harboured beneath the wet . . .) smack in the middle of Washington Square Park; one hand clutching at my fly, the other fumbling for change. The obvious was something hopelessly vacuous; perhaps it had something to do with The Boys Over There. The cold increased with every breath I took, glazing my lungs into brittle bags of blood. A terrifying enemy cranked the zealous handle on an Icy Machine and warmed to the task with every stroke. The park was winter bare with old skeleton fingers sticking from the trees. The earth was sick skin frozen to a corpse and the concrete tables upon which even in winter vacant men with snow banked to their ears played sullen games of chess appeared as loathsome toadstools that festered and broke from the dead flesh to feed on the oranged brains of lonesome men. The Arch celebrated some grand forgery and mass mutilation and squatted like a giant hunchback dripping with pigeon shit. The park looked as would the world after a hail of damnation had been vomited down upon it from the howling mouth of a diseased and helpless god. The wind swept it all with a dirty tinkle.

Happy! Happy, ye whirling bastards!

I stand here hated and spinning like a moss moon gathering the fungus of love. Affectionate malice is given me. The world is hushed and harpy at my movements.

There, yonder, over there on t'other side of the park is a man waving at me . . . the stick in his hand is a symbol of his good faith. And here, behind me, comes the friendly policeman on his beat who with great joy and peace of Christian Soul would happily batter my head down through my neck with righteous propriety upon outrage at my happy movements. Come, come, Tully, warm up your humours . . . wave back at the ruffian with the stick . . . greet the friendly fuzz.

"Good evening, Officer."

"What'n the hell you do'n after curfew? Was you expose'n yourself?"

"Why, not at all officer . . . I was just standing here

enjoying this bounteous park, viewing that magnificent arch over there . . . the most decadent of public monuments possible. Breathtaking . . . awe-inspiring."

One side of his face swelled in anger. "What'a ya . . . some kind of nut or someth'n?" An impossible question to answer . . . so many possibilities . . . so many directions to flee.

"I don't think so . . . but maybe . . ."

"What'a ya wave'n yer arms around like that if ya ain't some kind of nut or something?"

"I was just waving to a friend of mine over there." It struck me from an unexpected angle that I had to lie to the oaf to assuage his doubts on my sanity.

"Ya mean the guy with the stick?"

"Yes, that's right. Old Cecile. Always carries a stick."

He looked square at my left ear (museums full of pigs' bones!).

"Beep beep! Just old Cecile is it?"

"Huh?"

"Bow Wow!"

". . . ? . . . Did you say something?" He held one hand on his hip and the other extended toward me and limp at the wrist so that his hand dangled down like Madam Cafritz offering her finger-bones to the lips of a noble gent.

"Just old Cecile with his stick, eh? Oh that's niiith . . ." His voice squeaked into a lisping falsetto.

"I'm sorry," I said, "but it seems as if rapport has broken down here. . ."

"Woof. Woof!"

"Yeah, sure . . . go to it. Woof woof, as you say." I started edging away around the wading pool.

"Hold it there! Beep Beep!"

His eyes watered and went out as if his machinery had gone woo woo and plunged everything into darkness.

"CLANG!" he shouted out the side of his mouth and started around the wading pool after me. "CLANG CLANG!" he shouted, beating his nightstick on the edge of the pool. "Beep . . . BOW wow . . . Woof Woof . . . CLANG!" his entire repertoire as he circled around after me.

"Beep Cecile with his Woof-Woof stick . . . CLANG!" I had circled all the way around the wading pool to where I had a good view of The Monument. Cecile was still standing under the Arch waving his stick (comforting, I thought) . . . the park cold and maddened . . . the cop gaa gaa . . . Cecile waving his stick and I circling the pond. The cop suddenly stopped and stood stark-ass still, caught between the balance of his crazed sound effects and for a moment I thought he had slipped into catatonia, in which case I would have joyously grabbed his club and belted the shit out of him. Not so. He raised his stick with his left hand as if to throw it at me (awkward like a girl pitching a ball). I watched hand, stick and arm float there while all the flashing rings of his jeweled fingers snapped at my throat . . . with his other hand he pulled open the ruby buttons of his velvet and gold brocade coat and jerked a silver cannon out level with my belly button, the fine dutch lace of his cuffs hiding the striker-stone, wick and lock-levers of his shortened fowling-piece.

"Look out for the Moonlight!" I shouted and he whirled, dodging the quick moonbeams, screaming and waving his cannon at the yellow jelly dripping from the sky. "Glub glub Zap! Cecile's Stick Stuck! Heebee ho ho! Take that, you bastard! Woof woof!" he warbled, sending a stream of minnie-balls and lead sinkers smashing into the moon. I fumbled the plaster statue of Jesus out of me pocket and waved it at him and his face began melting and sliding down over his cravat, his shirt, his belt, his silken tights, his net stockings and trapped his shoes in a puddle of Mung! Oatmeal leaked through the widening pustules on his head . . . his hand dissolved around the handle of his gun and it dropped into the puddle of plasmic slime . . . a finger poked from his ear and withered as I watched . . . his coat caved in and the hair squirted in a tangle of escape from the top of his head. "OFAL OFAL OFAL!" I screamed and flung the statue into the palping mound convex of proto-jellification as it writhed and sucked at the frozen skin pressing at osmos with earth and grass and black stratums of quietude.

The gelatin spasms stopped and the bubbled surface

of the melted man leaked air and steamy vapors till the
dry transparent crust the snail leaves curl'd on the ground
had dropped away in the frost of my silent breath . . . safe
again! I looked across to the arch but Cecile was gone. I
closed my fly and left the park.

6.

Radix 3: Pain Increases With Action.

The silver edges too faked & honed, the nosebone shaped to receive Silver Balls of Neglect gathering there not to be called Snot but rather Booger Bits & Pieces or (for the geographically inclined) Buggers & Such . . . (brains . . . ears . . . ?) . . . it is as if the Feet were glued in the Shoes, the Shoes to the Earth, the Earth to the Sky, the Sky to the Universal Drip and there to the Vascular Saddle of Infinity and thus the Whole Phuking Shootin' Match forming a glistening stopper in Ole' Lonesome's ass.

If I were to write verse upon this theme I would start with:

Warriors . . . (water blades dipping)
The Swamp steaming with its viney drip . . .

Leak!
Hamper the Hunter!
Vipers twined about the twigs of futility . . .
An aged alligator injects his cock into
a hollow log . . .
Deceived! . . . defeated! . . .
there's no fool like an old croc . . .
(Disgusted with the Way of the Jungle but
unable to protest Tradition . . .)
Congestion of Ferns eating Man!
Embrace of Leafy Viciousness!

A band of Crazed Natives (an unfrocked Belgian Jesuit wearing only an old Spalding jockstrap with newt's teeth tells me with a wry smile, "Th' guv'm'nt tries to keep the Blacks from grow'n it but the people International Narco send out keep disappearing into the Bush as soon as they get a taste.") whoops through the Interior raping each bush and Crawly Thing in turn . . . a Boa Buggered! . . . Insects Had!

Or if I were bent toward The Drama I would ideomatically outline these philosophies in a Play thus:

Title: *LOOK MA!*   (In One Act)
Scene: In my backyard.
Time: During a ¾, eclipse of the sun (by the moon?)
Dramatis Personae: *A 274 lb. Mother* . . . (from upstairs)

. . . huge fatty arms and thighs loose and dripping down in pus-colored bags of skin . . . (her husband a drunken milkman with a light little asshole for a mouth and piss-ant eyes . . . told me the day I moved in downstairs (perhaps a warning?), ". . . in Oklahoma back in '27 I oncet whupt me an Indian, hayuf nigga he was, crost his haid wif a 22 single-shot ayund scatter'd hiz brayuns all over th' daince-hall flo' . . . th' layudies was stomp'n around in 'um for the raist o'th' nayit.")

Her 7 yr old daughter Deborah

Deborah: (looking up to where the sun should be) What makes eclipses Ma?
Mother: Go on back in the house and watch The Three Stooges!

(Curtain)

One might say the Ashcans of Disaster are full . . .

7.

Tully McSwine's New Cock:

... all this is to say that I (against tremendous odds) battered my way out of the park with God's Teeth snap'n at me ass at every step. The question I balanced on the mossy edge of expectation was: are my 3 Intelligences (my Sound, Sight & Locomotion) really an Autogamic Bundle of Blood, Bones & Boogers self-fertilizing and self-intersecting with Spontaneous Motion or is Ole' Lonesome really watch'n after my shaggy soul? ... that is, do I really (after all) perpetuate myself (O Immovable Object) with the Tully McSwine Theorum of Irresistible Horseshit? (... a Gandy has just Danced his way 6 feet up my anal canal and lodged himself midway in my Transverse Colon with a band of Chinese Coolies imported ostensively to hook up the President's Direct Pipeline with The Ladies' Home Urinal, but in actuality their purpose is to pounce on Tijuana from the north while Chaing Kai-shek invades

Mexico from the west . . . ! . . . Castro has been notified
. . . !)

Down the street I went.
What in the name of seven slobbering gods am I doing
so far from Home? Constant delusions of finding a cata-
lyst to set me abdicated and spinning through the whispering streets of America. Who-What-When-How, you
rusty blackguard? Rushing about to turn on the sirens
of the night! A Grand Picnic at Bethlehem . . . all the
inmates out eating cooked things in the bloated sunshine
. . . good! . . . prance among the dusty ruins in the morning sunlight . . . you'll never catch up . . . the world is
balmier than you, Tristram my son. Ofal . . . woof!

Down the block to Dolly's building. Cornelia Street
(". . . If for I want that glib and oily art . . ."). Up five flights.
Prepare a little speech, "OK, kid, now look . . ." Good. Rat-
atat-tat on the woody door. My ears hear scurrying about
in there. Knows me knock. Can always tell a man by his
knock or his cock . . . depends which side of the door yer
on. Come on strong . . . but forgiving. A crack of light
and an eyeball. "What'a ya want?" What's this? The Hairy
Voice of a strange man? Unfaithfulness afoot? Well now,
we'll see about that.

"From the power company. Come to turn off yer lights
. . . plunge ye into darkness."

"Who is it, Hank?" Dolly on the inside.

"I don't know. Some lame about lights." Menacing tone from that one. Look bad at him . . . give 'em a scare. I make a mean grimace.

"Well, get rid of him. Tell him I paid the bill."

"Look, she paid the bill. You got the wrong place, buddy."

"This is the residence of Miss Dolly . . . ?"

"Oh f'Chriiisake!" This from Dolly. She comes to the door.

"Now look, I've already . . . you son of a bitch, Tully . . . just what in hell do you think you're doing?"

"Good eve, dear Doll . . . and how does this brisk winter eve find thee? In the best of health and bodily comfort, I hazard to say."

"Goddamn it, McSwine! Just what in hell d'you want coming up here in the middle of the night?"

"Why love, I blush to say. Thoughtless of me. Should have phoned first, but then I didn't know you were having guests. May I come in?" sez I with one foot in the door.

"Hell no you can't come in! You can just turn around and march right back down those stairs!"

"I'll scream."

"Oh for the love of Christ, Tully, will you leave me alone?"

"Now what makes you think there's any passion to be squandered between the aforementioned gent and myself? Besides, I *have* left you alone. Figured you been punished enough . . . its cold out here." Poor old Hank lurking there behind Dolly, not knowing whether to shit 'er go blind.

"Let me handle this guy, Dolly!" Coming on very tough, that one. Starts to push past her so I reach down and grab an empty milk bottle stand'n outside the door.

"Come on out, you half-assed ape! I'll kick yer ass up a'tween yer shoulder blades so's you have ta take off yer shirt ta shit!" I could feel me nostrils begin to widen. He wasn't too sure now. He had the size, the weight and the reach, but I had the milk bottle. Dolly opened the door wider.

"For Christsake, come in here then, you idiot. Don't stand out there in the hall growling like a teen-age hood. You'll have me thrown out of the building." Poor old Hank stand'n there with his thumb up his ass knowing he's been aced out'a his nookie for tonight.

"Well?" She looked pissed enough to slash the ears off'n the sides o'me head.

"Look baby, could I see you alone?"

"Hell no you can't! I'm through, McSwine! I've had it! I've put up with all the cheap crap I'm going to take from you . . . you . . . you goddamn trick-talk'n monster!" There, she had it . . . monster. Yeah, Monster! . . . from beneath the deep . . . seaweed dripping from my ears . . . madness running from my eyes . . . the babble of ages running on my tongue . . . I was indefensible . . . a blot on the public welfare . . . a turd in the cookie-jar of a maiden's happiness.

"It was love what made me say those awful things," I whispered, husky like an emoting starlet, and cast me eyes to the floor.

"Love! Ha, ha, love! I like *that!* Love my ass, you bastard! Why all you know of love is that it makes you twitch between your legs! Don't talk to me of love, you walking erection!" (. . . it's only my short hairs you want to run your fingers through . . . never the noble moss growing on my mind . . . etc . . . I know . . . I KNOW! . . .)

"Dolly, baby, couldn't we talk this over alone? Just you and me? I mean there are things in our relationship that aren't meant for the ears of others." I smiled over at Hank as pleasantly as my rambling insincerity would allow. He frowned and put one numbed finger to his thickened brow. I looked back to Dolly . . . she was sneering at me, but ah . . . sweet slick sex was slithering behind her eyes . . . remembrances of my princely appenditure signal'd caution . . . the dear girl enjoyed adulterous copulation with my young self and fortunately she knew it.

"Don't be so corny, McSwine."

"Yeah, don't be so corny," Hank mumbled. I smiled . . . viciously . . . and thought 'Brilliant, my man . . . you've just ushered yourself out alone into the cold and darkly night!' Dolly turned to him and milked a little snake juice from the tits of her tongue.

"Say, man, why don't you shut your hole . . ." she hissed.

"Better yet, why don't you find a busy streetcorner and go grunt at the girls . . . hmmm?" If he'd had the balls he should have been born with he'd have rapped her up side the head a time or two, because there's no denying it . . . Dolly could be a piss-cut'n bitch and a half with damn little effort; but instead his ears got red and his vacant eyes began to water. Poor bugger, if I'd had a heart it would have bled all over my innards for him. Dolly just looked at him as if he was a bag of shit standing there . . . disdainfully, one might say.

"Well shitbird . . . you go'n a split?" That's one of the things I liked about Dolly, she always knew the right thing to say in strained situations . . . social graces and all that. He stomped over to the door and turned, shaking his finger at her (. . . if it was me I'd a shook my dick in her direction . . . the bitch!). "We've had it, you can bet your ass on that!"

"I never bet it, Hankie boy. Just as my sainted Mammy used to tell, 'Sell it or give it away, but never gamble with it' . . . later sonny." Slam! Zap! I thought the door was going to drip from its frame.

"You star-spangled bitch!"

"I know it."

"You didn't have to be so mean to the poor shit. After all, you probably snapped your snatch at him all night . . . by now he's probably the worst ambulatory case of

50

sexual frustration on the streets of New York . . . probably rape a tourist schoolteacher and make the morning headlines."

"It suddenly occurred to me that getting into bed with that primitive would have been asking too much of myself."

"You must have been getting hard up."

"From the looks of you I still am. When's the last time you bathed?"

"A week ago come next Tuesday . . . a mob of teen-age assassins attacked and pitched me into the East River . . . whilst I was floundering it came into my head to take advantage of the opportunity so I splashed around a bit . . . comes along a barge captain by name of Alexander Fix who figures I'm in difficult waters so he throws me a leaky lifesaver . . . hit me square on the headbone with the goddamn thing and it was glub glub from there till he got a boathook into my starboard armpit and pulled me aboard . . . must have looked like I was in rough shape because the next thing I remember he hit me with the surgeon and I went on the nod . . . that junkhead son of a bitch almost OD'd me right out'a this world . . . must'a figured I'd gone to meet The Man Beyond and threw me back because I came to in the deep spit'n ruptured rubbers and briny kotex . . . made me way to shore against overwhelming odds . . . mostly my inability to swim . . . I just inflated and floated in."

"The authorities ought to lock you up for your own safety, you goddamn kook. One of these days you're going to spin out and there won't be no barge captain to save your nutty ass."

"Welcome the day, Dolly me love, welcome the day!" I flopped down and settled back into a feathery bed with brass posts . . . damn thing come near to taking up the whole apartment. Her apartment was a dinky little two-room job on the fifth floor of a real funky building on Cornelia Street right smack in the middle of The Village . . . miserable place to live . . . tourists crawling out of the john for a turd's eye view of the local goings-on . . . you know . . . wild living . . . loose women . . . dope and despair . . . the standard myths the middle class use to slander us happy types with. Her shot was just dig'n that which was to be dug . . . scuffle'n and whore'n around . . . a bit of naked modeling for eatable goodies and to pay the rent and such comforts as will keep her fairly stoned . . . not a bad gig on the whole but still too many creeps use'n a charcoal pencil as an excuse to get a peep at a naked girlie. Our story was out of the old tradition: Boy meets Whore . . . Boy gets Clap . . . Boy gets 500,000 mg's of penicillin Right In The Left Cheek. I recover and Become a Poet . . . she gets the same treatment and Love was ours to do with as we would. You might say that in our relationship she was The Meat Gatherer while I stayed holed up in her pad—well-fed, fucked and suffering to Commit

Art. Once in awhile we fought and I would make a Grand Exit ("Fini!" I would cry as I gracefully tumbled down the stairs in my tubercular way) fleeing as was my wont to my dank pit of a room on the Lower East Side (I sodomized the landlady's cat in lieu of rent . . . she got her Thing out of it . . . the landlady, not the cat . . . poor puss didn't dig it at all) where I would spend the next week brooding over the more swinish aspects of love. Finally when the pressure at the head of my cock became too unbearable and carried me past the somewhat limited scope of mere masturbation I would limp back to a reconciliation that always blossomed into four or five hours of fevered fella-tio (the swallowing whole of The Tumescent Member) . . . Cunnilingus Off The Wall . . . hurried improvisations on anal eroticism and any form of acrobatic copulation to which we could at all bend our beatifically vile bodies . . . that is to say, we were orgiastic in our forgiveness.

The apartment was small, just two rooms and a crap-per. A big old-fashioned tub in which three grown men and a small boy could drown with relative ease was in one corner of the kitchen . . . the acre of brass-poled bed con-sumed most of the other room looking out east over the rooftops of Lower Manhattan. A crazy little fireplace that could boil the air faced the bed . . . boards clean scrubbed and polished bared the floor, and I suppose if one were given over to such things one could take one's meals there, but I hold it vulgar to eat off the floor. Cockroaches piped the hidey-holes and greasy crannies, multiplying at the rate of the municipal cockroach population squared every 17 seconds.

A very pretty genuine hand-painted Redon print of flowers all whirling in a happy maze was on the wall beside me. I looked at it . . . it looked at me . . . all those flowers whispering misty love words . . . the old gent must have sometime looked at life from the bottom of a mill-pond flat on his back among the fishes . . . sun slashing down through the water like gold and yellow stabs and spears . . . all the bright little flowers bo-peeping at him down there . . . nature coming to him like a Christmas tree through ground glass . . . his old rheumy eyes melting out all the lines that art has put to nature . . . diffusion of myths . . . energies transmitted from things in growth Right Before The Eyes . . . Tricks & Inventions shattered and gone behind as a hoot owl.

"My Sweet, did you cautiously throw out mention of a bath?"

"In defense of my sensibilities, I did."

"I stink from inability, not design . . . from innocence, not malice."

"You stink from want of a bath."

"The pulp and pips of my heart leak with purity."

"My nostrils suck embarrassment."

"Yea, but soapy spittle clogs my pump."

"Inexact odors shame my desires."

"Nobility of Vision laves my corruption of body."

"My Passion drags sooted from your fumes and vapors."

"You suggest . . ."

"A bath."

". . . a purgation . . ."

"A bath."

". . . of superfluities . . ."

"A bath."

". . . coated protection by . . ."

"A bath."

". . . which the perishable meat, raw and succulent, will be exposed to . . ."

"A bath."

". . . the withering air. You suggest . . ."

"A bath."

". . . an urging . . ."

"A bath."

". . . an exposure . . ."

"A bath."

". . . a repulsion . . . a vomit . . . a scraping . . . duty . . . an unrelenting scrub . . . a zealous cleansing of my hard-won accumulation of civilized sores & acnes . . ."

"A bath."

". . . for fear they will fester and erupt to contaminate your love-hole."

"Take a bath, liar!"

She filled the bath with gorgeous waters and perfumes while I peeled from my fetid threads like an ancient sodomite going down for the last time.

I was once a languid Pharoah slipping into a sea of silken pillows.

8.

& so the feather flies . . . depraved from the crib and
no help for that. Years of thrashing debauchery seeped in
behind my orbs. The bones of my cock clanked and ridged
in unblinking expeditions. The dry mouth mucoused and
convulsive. The cold nudity of room washed in bright
air around me turns the short hairs clinching inward . . .
curling helixes like black misshapen watchsprings . . . the
scrotum shriveled to a tight bag clutched and wrinkled
around the balls like fear . . . once from out the captured
heat of pants the long and beginning bloatation of fatty
cock still sponged against the possibility of penetration
now backs into itself shrinking into the pre-remembered
shroud of foreskin before the ax of circumcision scuttled
the brain's necessities . . . withdrawing into its own sick
folds to become just an inch of timorous and withered
flesh . . . just a light membrane rip of nausea curved across
the edge of one bewildered and anxious sphere.

The step into the tub: immediately a loosening . . . the

constricted cock unravels unhanded to allow its tip to
float gently out the water . . . the sack stretches and the
creases, tight cracks of corrugated flesh, smooth out to
allow the bag elongation weighted and hung down as if
by buttered stones . . . the spiraled hairs relax . . . small
and frequent warnings urge the unguarded cock to extension . . . it rises in petty jerks from the water . . . the
mouth gaping more to stare the onlooker in the eye . . .
the head rushed with blood to form an exact miniature
of the human heart . . . the whitened skin faintly flushed
pulls down in disrobement of a captive beacon . . . a slave
perched on stones and plunged into nakedness . . . now
. . . her own nakedness . . . low and the breasts hanging
down . . . threatening excellent precedence over my warty
tools . . . nipple and swollen gland kiss (the mouth-opened
tip glazed in the adhesion of transparent fluid) and slide
by so that a slight smeared glisten of pre-fluid turns a
brilliance to the dull brown redness of her nipple . . . the
exploded muscle hurrying through her soaped fingers,
taunting the inflated tube running beneath to channel the
translucent wash rushing . . . the bright puffs and bubbles of cleansing rinsed away . . . her lips clung indrawn
around bulging ridge . . . her teeth with strained control
jeopardize my cock's endurance . . . her mouth opens to
suffer the whole tubular swelling of my tumescent pain
and her rapid tongue works upward, drawing the final
spastic resistance into her mouth . . . an implosion first

forcing apart the vascular constrictions damming my semen, then raking convulsions chasing and taking and overpowering the one before as they pump my reluctant liquid up in great churns to be vomited out by a clogged and unsighting head howling for expurgation . . . the caps of sensation pulled tight and fastened over the opened brains . . . a balance of retina cross-hatching the sight . . . a quiet dying . . . her lips pull in final expectation to have it all and test my texture and viscosity on her tongue . . . in her throat . . . around the evasions of her passion . . .

(((Wait! how can I think clearly in the midst of an
　　orgasm?
　　wait wait the cornered wrinkles at my eyes turn
　　upward　wait　my mouth opens and my teeth show
　　a reflection (is it mine?) sprints into the
　　　　　　　　　　　　mirror
　　wait　for the space to clutch at my parts
　　　　　　　　　　　　　　　　I Said Wait!
　　　　　now wait I must wait again
　　　　　　　　　　　　　　& this part I know
　　　　must wait but cannot wait again
　　　wait wait wait wait wait wait wait wait
　　　　　　wait wait
　　　　　WILL OPEN IN MY HEAD!!!
　　　　　　　　　　　　　　　again now
　　must I repeat? All this sound is not necessary!)))

59

Having made my deposits into the orifice of my loved one I sink to the stale bottoms of reverie, submerging as I do so up to my earlobes, the better to contemplate the resemblance of Me . . . Rudy Vallee . . . God.

My time is your time, you bastards.

9.

McSwine Struggles Among The Spikes of Conjecture:

Why should I (having just had my root pluck'd by the incarnate of Anu's lustful goddess daughter Ishtar of Babylon and now laved up to my earholes in steamed and scented waters) be thought-filled by the vacant gestures of Rudy Vallee. I really cannot say why. All that I know of him is what I watched in my childhood movies and of my mother's flapper lust after him . . . megaphone, C Melody sax and all his nasal pipings of song. I attempt to draw theological analogies between him and God and achieve only a disbelief in the existence of either. Yet, I have seen him (as I have seen God . . . I who am so filled with Him/ He who is so filled with Me!), heard him speak, smile, could reproduce his cooing gestures . . . his nosey voice. Who is Rudy Vallee? Well, he was always a nice bumbling type chap who never quite made it . . . always the football hero's half-ass chum . . . belonged to the same frat as his

sweaty buddy but only because his folks were rich as shit
. . . always fell in the drink at boating parties . . . came
from a good home (money out the ass) so never had to
worry about the formation of an idea . . . girls all thought
him cute but he never got laid (that is, no dice except for
the loud brassy broad who organized things and who, at
the drop of a drunken suggestion, would have peeled into
the sack with even Acne Al she was so hard-up but like
nobody has eyes, not even Rudy who by this time must be
getting pretty fuck'n horny) . . . always the leader of some
Mickey Mouse band and singing through a megaphone
so's you can see his rancid tonsils . . . friendly (what could
he do?) . . . lots of shiny white teeth . . . dressed sort of
nutty (like 18 years behind the style, perhaps his only sav-
ing factor) . . . real simple in the head . . . always smiling
vacuously and ever the dupe for the chicaneries of the
slick-haired real rich prick who was going to grow up and
inherit the world and shit on everybody because like nobody digs him at all (sado-maso tendencies developed in
an over-competitive home . . . the pull of a constantly in-
disposed and frigid mother against the sneery rejection of
a sadist cocksman of a father who always thought the kid
was coming on a little too faggoty) and who (The Prick
I'm speaking of) usually ended up getting a blast from the
hero (a sweaty but handsome meathead dashing around
in a modest Ford Convertible and a sparkling jock-strap
that supported his nonexistent nuts) or a deft knifing by

the firm morality of a Young American Virgin from behind the unbreachable security of her padlocked vagina
. . . but as for Rudy, he was (as I said) everyone's dupe . . .
even the hero's when just a touch of that All-American
viciousness was needed to create a comic situation . . .
always good for the loan of his roadster . . . parents knew
he was an idiot but his mother insisted on keeping him
around as a constant reminder of the inadequacies of her
emasculated husband . . . poor Rudy . . . a sort of fifth-
string Great White Hope . . . stand'n around with his finger up his butt . . . can never really figure out what's going on so he just stands around and smiles. I could never
really understand what she saw in him, my mother that
is. She was also (I think) flip for John Garfield, but then
Shit! So was I . . . a tough bastard really, but like gentle
. . . the whole shot precluded . . . never actually had much
of a chance . . . they were out to nail his ass from the start
. . . they knew it . . . he knew it . . . hell, everyone knew
it but he was going to wail his nuts off in the meantime.
Came from the other side of the tracks . . . had a nice
old white-haired pie-bake'n muff for a Mom and a night-
watchman type daddy who lived in a scabby but neat
little shack down where the trains went woo woo. Chicks
always dug him . . . he got terrible hung up on chicks . . .
and poverty. Always some rich chick trying to lead him
away from the simple life and get him all fucked up . . .
and always a lot of bad cats hang'n around with their easy

money ("Just this one job Jim and you'll be able to buy that big house up on the hill for your Ma where she'll be as good as anyone . . ."). Three types of women in his life (that is excluding his Mom who, we get the idea, didn't fooosh him out of her woooomba but rather found him under the elderberry bush in the backyard): First there was this poor-but-honest workin' girl who didn't hit the sack with no one until some stud went in hock up to his nubs to lay the 10-carat churchy bit on her . . . second was the rich dame who lets him sweat on her some and maybe get a little stink finger before her Daddy (who owns the world) auctions her off to some racy bunch with eight-year-old hooch and polo ponies . . . (. . . beside the world her old man also owns the railroad next to the tracks of which is the creepy little ruin in which the old folks tremble, and for whom and on whose time John Garfield's Old Man has been featherbedding for the past forty years in liverish expectation of a tin watch and a limited credit card at the company store and if John don't stop grab-ass'n with Sinful Cynthia (who is like really a sexual cripple because of a weird shot with a pack of Dalmations at the age of 12, and like who can't come . . . dig?) he, *her* old man, will frizzle his Old Man's ass right out a gig three minutes before his pension is due) . . . third and last is the tough chick . . . the gang moll maybe who's been shat on all her life . . . used by one stud after another . . . sent out to hustle by her Ma when she was still just a wee bit of a whore. She loves him and lays him because she knows that in this racket ya gotta take what ya want before it's too late or ya get aced out'a it, or something like that . . . he lays her and leaves her for the sweet chick with the Untouchable Tits who comes on like she don't even know where her snatch is (and who like in real life is a terrible junky), and by then we know that she (the tramp-with-a-heart-of-gold with whom, even John, everyone has come on like a miner) has got to Get It In The End because she did a whole raft of raunchy things like screw'n and drive'n the getaway car, but she is a slightly good apple in a bad barrel and so she gets it in the guts from the mob when she throws herself in front of John as some terrible bad bastard tries to blast him with a Cleveland piano from the back seat of a big black Buick that goes screeching off into the tarry night . . . and he holds her head while she bleeds all over his Florsheims and tells him to take Betty With The Undiscovered Cunt and Go Straight and then checks out right there on the sidewalk as Betty Bubbles and the Blossom Maids (who have just come out of the candy store, in front of which the slaying took place, where they were buying ice cream for a little Methodist bacchanal that's going on in the crib down by the freight yards where the old white-haired muff and the Old Gent live) breaks into a chorus of "It's a Groove When You Move," and Betty (in a gushy bellow intended as a whisper) says, "She loved you John. She loved you as I love you, for the good that's in you . . ." and her voice trails off as she computes his potential earning power . . . Fade Camera as John and Betty split hand-in-hand just in time to prevent the quart of ice cream from tearing through the bottom of the wet soggy paper bag and into the pool of blood that has leaked out of the Punctured Prostitute right in front of a group of oafs who have come out from the candy store to gawk at the stiff . . .

*   *   *

ODE TO JOHN GARFIELD

John Garfield is Strong Brother

John Garfield snarls tough like a tiger

John Garfield never wore no necktie

John Garfield built my first 12 years

John Garfield bid me weep in the trees of my 1930's

John Garfield sneers and punches Assholes around

John Garfield hard vagabond cat walk'n down the
    tracks with yer jacket over yer shoulder hold'n onto
    it with just one finger in the collar

John Garfield share'n stew with the Bo's and pass'n his
    last smokes around

John Garfield swing'n off a boxcar in the big city and
    don't give a fuck who sees him

John Garfield tramp'n down the highway and stop'n
    to change a flat on a Lincoln for a chick with class

and a sweater full'a tits

John Garfield meet'n her polo play'n brother and his
snake friends with pencil moustaches and not take'n
none'a their high-toned crap

John Garfield meet'n her mother who don't dig him
because he ain't their type but he don't give a damn
and don't take no crap from her neither

John Garfield be'n offered a fancy job by her international banker father and not take'n it because HE
DON'T TAKE NO CRAP FROM NOBODY

John Garfield breath'n all over the rich chick in the
grass on a hill beside the roadster under the trees
with the top down (& her fling'n her legs up around
him!)

O JOHN GARFIELD (died of an OD in bed with a
crawl'n nympho . . . !)

PUNCH'N THE WORLD RIGHT ON ITS ASS!

*   *   *

. . . and I gritting my teeth in a dark movie palace . . .
The Gate . . . a fleahouse on Bridgeway in Sausalito '37—
'38—'39—'40 . . . get in for 11 cents if you was under 12
. . . go down and get in line at 12:30 Saturday noon and
grab-ass with the other kids till 1:00 when they let you
in (Sneed the manager . . . a real cocksucker who was always boot'n me out because in Big Fight Scenes I'd get
real excited and yell, "Kick 'em inna balls!") . . . and then

on my way home alone after a double-feature w/news-reel—short subjects—previews of coming attractions—cartoon & flash-card-advertisements . . . trying to stretch the ten-minute walk home up the windey streets along the buckeye trees into a half-hour . . . fighting and sneering (sun glint on my rugged jaw) through the empty streets full of bad bastards (cops & gangsters alike) . . . snub-nosed .38 in one hand and punch'n out Assholes with the other as the 5:00 hills sent shadow fingers across the bay to Oakland . . . remembering how John Garfield hid in a culvert as the feet of the heat went right by his face, almost tripping in his breath . . . up Princess Street into Bulkley . . . ducking into mossy gates and crouching low and running behind ivy-clung fences . . . rapping out the used shells from my gun and reloading as I hunkered down behind scrub-oaks . . . pitching buckeye grenades down into willow-hidden O'Connell's Beach where years later I gulped embarrassed gasps of night and sticky hair as my frightened fingers tugged elastic and silk that covered her still near-bald mons veneris of puberty . . . mysterious imagined knowledge . . . and to both our infinite and fantastic surprise a finger somehow slipping between her underpants and her rounded unopened split & for an instant a horrifying paralysis . . . ('. . . . *My God . . .*
. . . . *I touched her cunt!*') . . . stricken! with humiliation and misery (but later in bed I lay staring at the moon thinking about *It* . . .) and wondering if I could face her

68

Monday in school (15 years later she telling me that even
going to school Monday was almost impossible, thinking I would tell all my tough chums . . . ha ha, as if I even
dared whisper it to my own secret ear! . . .) . . . then shock
of recognition blasting us into an embarrassed scramble
to straighten our hot and tangled clothes trembling . . .
(& O O O how my balls ached on my way home!) . . . sure
I would faint under a streetlight . . . trying to tear a picket
from a fence, this to relieve my bursting scrotum from
the tightening fist of imagination: a high-school reme-
dy from Frankie Andermahr and Leroy Holmes . . . Big
Make-Out Artists . . . O how I used to believe those bastards . . . sit in class and peep my fanciful lust upon those
adolescent teasing virgins who, Frank and Lee swore on
their manhood, *Put Out*, and how in torment (at night/
in bed) I scrambled the ladders of my Inadequacy miserable that I could not leisurely swim in a Sea of Sex (&
for a whole year between the ages of 12 and 13 I became
a compulsive masturbator . . . jacking off every night for
a year . . . crying because I couldn't keep my hands off of
it . . . sure that my shame screamed out of my eyes at my
father as we sat down to breakfast each morning . . . sur-
er still when the Sure Sign of acne ("Hickies," "Zits" and
"Poolops" they were called to my never-ending horror)
gripped my face, and still I could not leave off (for a short
period when I was sixteen I was called "Pus Face," but not
for long as the caller would get a belt in the mouth . . . not

that I was that tough that I could whip anyone, but that I would *fight* anyone who said it and so it couldn't even be dropped in jest . . . it's a drag having to fight over a joke . . . even getting my first fuck . . . Gad! . . . if there were only some way to get around that first fuck . . . it's a wonder we're not *all* sexual cripples from the horror of that first fuck . . . Sunday afternoon out fart'n around Russian River in Frank Roberts' '46 Ford . . . Frank driving, Skeeter Wright in the front seat next to him, me being a gangster in the backseat and peer'n toughly out the window at the peaceful citizens . . . both of them older'n me (Frank 17—Skeeter almost 17—Me 15) and had Had It lots (they said) of times (which was pure horseshit) . . . anyway, cruising through Rio Nita (little river resort town) we spot Kathy ("Gangbang") K. and stops to see if she'd do it . . . The car door opens and Skeeter gets out, punches me in the arm again and whispers, "Hurry up . . . make it." I get in and close the door. Kathy is sitting up in the back seat trying to pull her twisted pants over her bare thighs . . . that's all she has on . . . just her unbuttoned blouse, no bra, and those small white twisted pants halfway up her thighs. I just sit there looking at her . . . the small flat breasts through the unbuttoned blouse . . . the faint blondish wedge of hair where she held her legs together . . . the terribly twisted pants just a few inches over the bend of her knees . . . she stopped struggling with the pants and looked at me. "Can I do it by hand?"

she said. I sat shuddering, stunned and sagging . . . Oooo
Jesus Christ what was happening? "No," I said simply,
"no."

No I didn't want her to do it by hand . . . I wanted
the real thing so I could lift my head up in a company
of squirming boasters leering through their acne and say,
"Yeah, sure . . . I've had a piece of ass," and know that I
wasn't lying through my teeth. But then . . . it was gratis
. . . should I mention her methods? "No," I said again,
electric paralysis ridged in my bones. "You never did it
before, did you?" she said as if she were trying to help me
get it started . . . not putting me down . . . no humiliation
intended . . . just a question intended to find out if I knew
what to do. My first intellectual response urged me to
protect my status as high-school braggadocio and swag-
ger through the whole sordid mess with feigned wisdom
. . . but . . . I could just miserably mutter "No, " and wish
I was someplace else far away where such considerations
were unnecessary . . . . where sex itself was unnecessary.
She smiled kindly (what a gorgeous human she was, I
think now, though I'm sure I hated her then . . . it is a very
fortunate fellow who ever took her to wive for him) and
turning from me she slid those twisted pants off and lay
back on the seat.

With ghastly ineptitude and swollen fingers I managed
to fumble out of my clothes and trying not to look at her
I stumbled down on top of her and lay there stiffly. It was

she who reached down and tried to guide my frightened
cock . . . I could do nothing but stare out into the sunny
forest with frozen eyes . . . (I could hear Frank and Skeeter shrieking their heads off outside the car and thought
vaguely they must be watching). "You come quickly," she
said. Again horror . . . horror compounded . . . horror
dominating as the current rate of emotional exchange. I
looked down and saw that as she held my cock tightly up
against those very young mons veneris I had indeed . . .
surely had . . . without any doubt at all . . . I had . . . un-
questionably come, yes . . . yes, undeniably I had unloos-
ened my gummy wad in her hand, over the soft curved
Mound of Venus, into her scant and pale pubic hairs, but
could it legitimately be called . . . be considered . . . a fuck?
That was important . . . I had not actually penetrated into
her, but the proximity? . . . that must count for something!
I thought I could justify it into a bona fide fuck, for after
all there were no rules covering the depth of penetration
nor penetration at all as far as I knew . . . wasn't the old
maxim, "A fuck's a fuck," applicable in all cases regardless
of whether you went in cock, balls, asshole and elbows or
just gently nudged it with the blind eye? The strange thing
is that I felt nothing, neither in a tactile sense nor in the
ejaculation of orgasm stuff . . . absolutely nothing. If she
had not called my attention to it I would not have known
that I had had an orgasm . . . there was only my milky evidence to show for it. "I'm sorry," I said helplessly . . . God

how ridiculous it all was! "Oh," she said with a friendly little smile as she vacantly examined her damp hand. "Oh . . . don't worry about it. It'll be better next time." Next time? There was never going to be a next time! Why next time? If this is what it was, what reason would there be for a next time? I had had my "piece of ass" and could boast among the others . . . I could think of no reason that would entice me into a next time . . . none at all . . . much rather would I fantasize and masturbate at leisure in the hot secret nudity of my own bedroom. I was (I thought) forever excused from committing this grotesque . . . unsensational . . . awkward . . . nothing. I had "done it" and that was enough to satisfy the rigid social demands of puberty. I had had it . . . enough and goodbye forever to this painful stuff. I saw no possible reason why a man could not live out his life by his own hand . . . gaaaa, later . . . much later on "next time."

Funny thing is that a year and a half later I traded a brand new khaki uniform shirt the army had just given me to an Okinawan prostitute in exchange for "next time" in a matted bed of saw-grass overlooking the stepped and moon-shimmering rice field of Chinen Plateau and after it was quickly over (although much more successful than the "first time") I lay there watching the cold East China Sea wondering on Kathy K. . . . wise goddess harlot in her youthful instruction.

O John Garfield!
Life loved . . .
my hard Hero & Handsome . . .
proletarian vagabond . . .
Look, your lessons blossom!

10.

"Say, you going to stay in that tub till you're just a soggy bag of wrinkles?" I twist about in the tub and behold Lovely Dolly with the heaving bosoms.

"I was just laying here in this collapsible bath thinking on what to do with myself . . . my life that is."

"Just don't do it when I'm around."

"You're lovely."

"Stuff it."

"No . . . really, I'm melting with sincerity."

"It's not your sincerity that interests me."

"That's all I've got to recommend me to your love'n arms."

"You've got a lot to recommend you, but it's got nothing to do with sincerity . . . unless of course that's the code name you've given it."

"You belittle me."

"Not with that thing I don't."

"You flatter me."

"It's not flattery friend. It's, shall we say . . . a feeling I have for the thing."

"If you like. I begin to think it's only my body you're after."

"You sound like a high-school whore, McSwine. It seems I can remember pulling that one a few times."

"You've more originality than that."

"I've learned a lot since graduation."

"True, true . . . academic circles can be limiting."

"Yeah . . . ivory towers."

"Ivy-covered walls."

"Rose-colored glasses."

"And some not-so-ivory towers."

". . . cracks in the walls . . ."

". . . and in the glasses . . ."

". . . cracked glass walls . . ."

". . . and towers . . ."

". . . dying ivy . . ."

". . . and moldering roses . . ."

". . . the ivory chipped down for bookends and paper-weights . . ."

". . . old bidets and thunder mugs . . ."

". . . smashed by turbines of chrome and dynamos of steel . . ."

". . . pitiless exposure under the historic leer of neon . . ."

". . . set upon . . . shat upon . . ."

". . . eroded by the waves lapping from a sea of piss . . ."

". . . moss entrails clinging . . . spangled with old crab eyes . . ."

". . . split . . . splintering . . . parting from the skull in great shales to slither and drop beneath the yellow waves . . ."

". . . an ivory bottom to the sea . . ."

". . . waiting beneath the fishes . . ."

". . . and the end not to come . . ."

". . . waiting there for an endless coming . . ."

". . . while here we come without end . . ."

". . . ended by our coming . . ."

". . . of unended come . . ."

". . . coming endlessly . . ."

11.

Dolly, in brownish moments, might be full of preaching about the way I dragged my ragged carcass around this dusty globe, but in her preaching she was minister to the flesh.

She rubbed me all over with a great woolly towel big enough to fly as a flag from the tip of the world. I could love this girl and take her to wive for me if I thought my ways of bumping into the scrambling beauty of life wouldn't be curtailed, but the ways of keep'n girlies up to their nubs in lov'n and such just isn't compatible with the waving of arms and legs and the shouting at distant figures that I had to do . . . too many check points and balances established in the politics of love.

Lord love you girl! Dolly wrapped the towel around me and I stood smiling clean and silent like a sort of blizzard-eyed monk in whom the creep of doubt has picked and bored the brain to let seep and leak away the more militant aspects of the mortification of the flesh.

I settled back in her great soft bed and watched her build a fire and set match to it. Great danc'n flames and shadows! The only light in the room came from the blaze, and Dolly stood tall in it with her black hair gripping her shoulders and a wide black leather belt hugging her waist. O Jesus Saints & Sinners . . . I wanted to love my Dolly till the sun went green and the night turned tricks on the moon's long beams! (. . . but but but O jazzed-up totem, for how long?)

Chilly fingers tapped at the window. Tiny coins of snow drifted past the panes like they had been poured from God's frosty money bag. I was covered with the bells of peace and love. Silver chimes rustled in my hair. Out over the night I could hear the muffled sponges of life rattling through the slush of the city.

This I know . . . Pain Increases With Action . . . but damn me I must ask thee, who can bear the painless stance of purity? Millions I suppose, or so it has been demonstrated. And if you dance and gesture on the edges of civilization watching the political acrobatics of confusion spill reason melted for the belly's sake down over the sides of disaster so the stuff slides along the streets. engulfing Folks . . . Nations . . . Worlds . . . Eternities . . . what then O Lonely Lamp Post? Is one any farther In or Out of Wisdom? Does one stand any closer to the Joyous Gods breathing one to the other? Do I be Fool leering at the dancing piano of life? . . . the goodies plucked from all about me on the hard rock streets while I sit impaled and dazed like a captured bandit on the mirrors of my righteous poverty? Do I become stuffed with fear and urge sentimental questions?: "Dolly, my only love, will you be my bride?" and risk the deballment of a terse "Nope."

"Why the hell not?" (I told you to watch out for anger.)

"Because you don't mean it." (Simplicity itself.)

"By the eyes of Jesus I do!" (Lie you bastard . . . Lie!)

"Maybe you do . . . right now. You're warm and a little drunk and it's cold out on the street and in a little while it will be nice to crawl all over each other, but in the morning you'll wake up shouting that you want God's Golden Fishes for breakfast and I won't be able to supply you with them." (Sweet Suffering Reason! . . . I've had enough of Reason! Treacherous Reason! Insidious Reason! Insufferable Betrayer of Lies!)

"Goddamn it Dolly, I love you!" (Ha Ha, methinks the Foole . . .)

"Sure, and I'll be your lover, Tully, but not your wife. I don't think you really want a wife . . . you want a captive who'll slip placebos to you whenever the cold fingers settle around your throat and your paranoia begins jumping up and down. You don't really want to draw anything from me except perhaps a few sexcoated gumdrops to keep your nuts from aching. I'm sorry baby, but it's your shot, not mine."

She was sad, my friend, and I was down . . . down like

the sunshine diffused on the floors of the sea . . . sad and down . . . not with the way we wanted things but with the way we wasted them. It's just as old Uncle Billy Burroughs says: "Nobody owns life, but anyone who can pick up a frying pan owns death." I loved . . . what? . . . Dolly? . . . yes . . . and my own glistening innards . . . that too, yes . . . and a spectral burst of desert flowers I once saw in the chill New Mexico dawn . . . love for flowers . . . yet I just loved, only loved and all that past the now is still to be loved . . . new discovered mechanics of myself? . . . new Dollys? . . . undiscovered flowers? . . . what love? . . . has love loved?

She stood in the firelight dropping her wrappings like a Druid maid going up to the welcoming sacrifice. What could I do but watch as the mouths of sex hummed from every fold and mound? Bending to my taste, hunched and straightened, jig-sawed and fitted like a fleshy puzzle, sex slithered over us like a naked spider.

12.

. . . This mark (!) & this . . . signal: I Dream In Fearful
Numbers . . .

Somewhere down in the far angry hollow of my mind
I was a desperate young wanderer, and as I stood now
watching the sea throw its arms back and forth like an old
mourner in a life of Sundays I felt as if in my gun hand I
held the black rubber plug snatched from the ugly suck-
hole way down at the bottom of the sea, and as I watched
. . . the whole fill of ocean whirl'd down the drain to
plunge and hiss onto the Fires of Fear.

13.

Dawn laid a white glove over my face and I awoke to a taut blue sky and a city swollen with snow. The feathers on my eyes made ragged edges on the brilliant light that hurried through the panes. I closed my eyes again and ducked my head back down into the fleshheated bed. Dolly lay still-tossed, her relaxed body breathing among the sponges of sleep.

14.

Not this, not that. A last overpowering plunge of snow
. . . indecisive tight-lipped days neither spring nor winter. But the snow doesn't make it. Attacking in the lull of
night it opened its white cisterns and let fall its all . . . but
it just doesn't make it . . . as if doomed. It is as if during
the night the arbiter of seasons had hiked back over the
lip of dawn to tip off the sun to what the snow had done,
and so in the morning up comes a big blasting orb wal-
lowing around in a bitter blue sky . . . spitting spears of
heat . . . the cold cushy mounds wasted . . . dirtied . . .
flung about by muddy wheels . . . folks stepping in it . . .
kids building fires in it . . . rats dripping rat turds in it . . .
Puerto Ricans throwing salt and sand on it . . . (I see an
old juiced-out gent in orange galoshes pissing into it
from a third-story fire escape, the yellow line arching
and steaming down to follow itself into a black and
melting piss hole far below him) . . . two well embalmed
and whiskered wanderers found dead in it frozen at the

84

final end of unnumbered soupy salvations . . . yea! san-
ctified sadness freezes in it . . . . It Melts . . . . I tell you,
IT MELTS & IS GONE!! and then (perhaps) s p r i n g
c o m e s
(the orgasm weakened)
             & then
      ACTION IS HAPPENING
                        the shift of the breeze . . .
         the sun/Mumbling

   I can hear it . . . on the street . . . moving in all directions. The Young Assassins are out . . . careful . . . circling
. . . cautious . . . pinning each other with dirty eyes . . .
razors sewn in their hatbands . . .

      WATCHING THE STREET / The action
      Electric cafés   chrome green candy stores
        (Jewel' d Music Machines!)

firemen languid with their hoses . . . The Heat sweating
inside their Revolvers . . . breathing beneath oversized
hats, bogus hats, shoes, underwear, dirty suits, spy-type
trench coats . . .

Grass the color of piss disrupts the parks (. . . a waiting fantasy cracks the sly wrinkles at the corners of my
eyes: shall I release my slobbering pack of hounds to
eat and gobble the hunkered old folks taking their daily

bitterness in the park . . . chew them into the arms of a well-deserved death?)

Spring limpid like a queer magician spitting birds . . . hidden birds teetering in the trees, watching from the buildings.

Action is happening/hovering, shrill meals explode . . . death's sandwich revolving . . . Action sweats a warning—a sign in a dark window:

Madame Blank will read your photograph.

Dolly and I walking (Her Sex fondles my damnation!) down East 2nd toward Peter and Allen's, (The Action standing near us) past the firemen, past the bad cats in porkpies capturing the doorsteps . . . their eyes on her/all over her/their eyes fucking messages of her inside their heads . . . I Look Hard . . . my shades blot out the speed of my iris . . . Action swift in my Brain . . . we move on/ Quickly. Somewhere behind us (On The Street!) the distant breathing of brutality:

Barbara Gee, age 14, flees down Avenue D. Angel Torris, age 16, gold earring ripped from his punctured ear, bleeding real blood and curses screaming,
"Burn 'em . . . BURN 'EM!"
. . . a bullet kisses in the back of her head.

*   *   *

Action Is Grass:

Cannabis Sativa/a charred seed blossoming between The Eyes.

A Scene . . . this Image crumbled into ritual: We meet Hunk in the hall, a greeting in the rooms (light-years of salutation pass imperceptible . . . passion leaked all emphasis from the Signal.) Peter is slow, feeding his cats, his intelligence concentrated on the hunger of 5 witch-black kittens . . . the kitchen walls a puke green . . . fibers worn brown in the rusted oilcloth . . . cups, old breakfasts, dirty books, & a frozen picture postcard from the South American Jungle where Peter's friend lingers shouting his poems at Concepción.

Dolly hands me from atwinkst her bosoms Ziz Zag & Stash & we take a Trip . . . a gentle journey beneath the scalp . . . (ah, soft you there . . .)

Mine/not so gentle:

> Boil'd Meat!
> Wet Bread!
> Spoons left in Food!
> The Breakfast of Hate Revolving . . . !)

Hunk/hugging his comfort, reads aloud hisonlypub-
 lishedstory:

> It is about: a homosexual hermaphrodite
> Who also happens to be: a junky
> Who has: 3 puppies
> There is: a Bust
> The Heat squashes: 1 of his puppies
> & he melts into: a medical document certifying
> his condition . . . .

a very hard type story . . .

iron understatement right down to the last scream.

Peter fondles his cats. Lafcadio is silent/unshaven (this
morning from Leo, a letter: ". . . I have had my head
shaved, inside and out . . . I would say a tonsured saint
but have been known to wobble.")

                                                      and lying
amongst a soiled bed, a stripped pillow atop his head. I
think to ask him to chess, but when we play he smiles at
the chessmen . . . a secret rapport like only he was playing. His father (a mysterioso figure) lives in an uptown
hotel & L. goes on the Tubes to play midnight games
with him . . . his battered board under one dusty arm . . .
his pieces in a brown paper sack.

                        Bless him!

                              (& I smile & show my teeth)

& am Glad! Yea Glad he rises up unspoken . . . O Blessed
Gladness such majik yclept him Lafcadio!

    No! Danger & Such involved in chess . . . lose my
way . . . never get out
                drop my identity among the pawns
get captured by a slick Bishop
                    charged by a lumbering Knight
smashed by a silent Rook
                    (cornered by a Quick Queen!)
                        Later.

Jarry enters . . . (A's directions of him: "He giggles on
street corners.")
    "Up yers!" I sez.
    "Up my what?" sez he.
    "Precisely!" sez I.
Exit Jarry . . . (amid a frenzied counting of the public
dead.)

                *   *   *

Action Oils The Street:

The Afternoon hammers its Golden Fist against the window (. . . to be granted the license to: STAND AT A WIN-
DOW & LOOK DOWN!)

I ask for a book, "Have you a book?" Pete looks square at me & bends among the books. "Yeah, I got a book . . . somewhere."

Dolly (moving that body) says she is going to split, see me later, yeah, later she to see me & I her later when I have hobbled home to open the windows at the night and we to lean together naked on our bed watching the incredible screeching painful sex of alleycats move across the battered backyard beneath our window as if they were copulating with Hidden Razors, and I will lay amongst her thighs in the light from across the yard, above the cats, a bare lightbulb dangling in the building there where a lonely man paints his room red, working slowly in his red room like a stark mime (her tongue flutters on my privileged flesh) in the shadows from his light, and I will hear a voice from his strangled lightbulb, from his red room, a choking voice caw broken swallowing, reminding me of a gull I saw once at sea from a ship, a gull lunging at the waves in hunger as we lunge at our years (and in the dawn I will smell the faint odor of her comfortable female lust).

Peter hands me a book with a red & black cover. Opening, in the book, I find this:

"The Mask! Lo, the mask!
Spitting wilderness venom

over New York's imperfect despair!

December 1929"

Action moves a page/a message waits:

> This is April month/April 1960
> & I am 27 & ½ years in this poem,
> in this city now where Lorca was.

I must balance or I will fall into the mouth of a poem.

Lorca
a murdered poet
German rifles in Spanish hands
knocking him to the old cruelty of dust
grinding his beautiful tongue
dragging him from his house
the Falangistas splitting him
letting the terrible silence of his fountains
the flood of his anguished coffins
his bitter columns
plunge with his Blood
into the ancient pre-Moorish streets of Granada
August 1936

* * *

THE POET LIVES WITH THE PAPER BIRDS OF DEATH FLUTTERING ABOUT HIS EYES

*   *   *

I have thought of the numbered fullness of moons
& of Love

*   *   *

Action Implied/using time:

You must wait with it . . . in It.

I squander goodbyes, move to the street and walk watching the edge of my hours slide along the gutter. I pass an old man in a doorstep and he raises his arm as if to ward off the violence of my greeting. At a fruitstand I stop and buy tangerines, remembering Lew Welch tell of walking 14 blocks in the blast of a New York summer 8 years ago to buy a bag of tangerines and walking 14 blocks back to his room to eat them and finding that all/ all were rotten and he could not.

Action is an image falling into Old Time:

If I . . . Stop! If I . . . NO! Now . . . if I enter my rooms (Stale & Hot), move to open the window.
(in bewildering moments the montage reversed like

Cocteau's Eurydice falling *up* from the bed . . .)

A breeze suffers my room, billowing my curtains.

15 years ago/in San Francisco/standing on the high edge of Fillmore Street that tipped down into the Bay sheer like a paved cliff falling away before me, I watched the bleached spinnakersails ballooning on the bay, a bright Sunday morning crisp as chips & blue as meadows, the whitecaps running outnumbered by sails.

> I then a watcher in a blue day . . .
> watching spinnakers then.
> The clouds do not refuse to move.

*   *   *

Action leans out of Memory:

I can remember as a child washing before dinner, drying my hands hard and well, not wanting to touch the white cotton bread with wet hands, and recall certain phrases, "Do not leave spoons in food!" (the Ear sending out tentacles of cautious feeling), "Do not drip wax on your toes!" (sitting hidden in the backyard bushes dripping red candle wax on my bare dirty feet) . . . Flashes of Infant Orgasm . . .

(do I imagine this/hopefully?)

Action Jabs The Thoughtless Cycle of The Eye!

I inspect a tangerine . . . it is not rotten and I feel I have been cheated . . . Yaaaa! Where is My Mother's Tongue now? & History? & the 5 black kittens? The Visionary Leaf? Dolly & The Moving Spoons of Sex? & Lorca? Yes . . . what of Lorca?

VAGUE ASSAILANTS INTO WHOSE INNARDS MY ARMS HAVE SUNK!

I tell you it is *not* the Light what gathers on The Eye, it is the glare . . .

THE GLARE!

(Action is Happening . . .)

15.

Night came in summers once to spread its vague fingers across the face of town . . .

To begin with then: A Lyric . . . a song twisting . . . a sound of soft insanity in the fall of leaves. Wait! I see no fine Italian hand. Some help . . . your arm if you please . . . or perhaps your tongue. I tell you I need some help if I am to continue . . .

I come to think of Action as a season of prewritten History. History: a mechanical incantation upon the vanishment of youth death Glory! . . . a disheveled epidemic of unruly time . . . a chronic mold of civilized diseases. (Maximus Olson sez, "History is the memory of Time.")

O Unrolled Space of America! It is not so much for the vanished red Indians & Phantom of buffalo, the gunshots whipping express ponies & coaches that we worry our memories for, it is Space Left Behind, disappeared from empty holes of time gasping in the past from whence ancient things have fled before our measurements began.

Listen! I once traveled 3000 miles to a place where 185 years ago some men trying to found a True Republic threw some tea . . . perhaps I misunderstood.

I am trying to tell you . . . what? . . . this: I have stood at the exact spot Juan de Fuca is thought to have landed from an old boat 3 or 4 hundred years ago, and waved my arms in a dignified gesture much the same as I thought he might have done & Nothing Happened!

(History fading away like hot messages written in onion juice!!!)

Damned & Doomed we are to clutch at the vapors of Histories fading and misting from our thoughts between our ages . . . nothingness full of form and exactitude, weights & heights, Measurements, precise actions, distances & dues, causes & disasters, our lives consequences of What Is Past & Now Gone, 5000 years of sweat and semen scraped from the body of man and thrown to the earth! Everything for The Earth! Do Not Think Upon It! If only we could keep from thinking upon what we have done . . . but we cannot stop, strenuous wants clack clack clacking all thru the humid halls of History, our brains flapping out thoughts on what might have happened if nothing had happened . . . if nothing will happen . . . is happening . . . and so, on to the greeting and surplus salutations: "What's Happening?"—as if anything could happen! (shrinking from the answer . . .) to deconfuse What Has Happened from What-Has-Gone-Down-Before! If only History could swallow itself as it happens and leave us unknowing and unconcerned to be dazzled by that which is Just Before The Eye . . . (I think of Mad Jack scribbling The Planets in a northern fourth-floor cell . . .) . . . but not to be! In the stead of Sight revealing That which The Eye can See, we grip History limpid like a forgotten flag and wave it to suppress our own ghosts . . .

* * *

PLANET'S BLOOD & DRAGON MEAT

(A Utopian Lecture)

I.

Praemissa

REVOLUTION (A Politic/a History) &
Junk (a Medicine/a Vision)
The Sword & The Spike.

The Revolutionary fixes the Body Political upon the same Time-Table Of Sickness that tolls the Junky's fix to the Body Physical . . . *clear proof.*

The Fit (the Works, the machinery) is translatable into a ready accumulation of Historical Principles and Dialectic . . . *proof presumptive.*

Causation: Disenfranchisement and/or Suppression of Political
Gesture:
&
On the Street/The Score-The Burn-The Roust-The Bust/The Scuffle!

Reaction: Injustice to the Flesh becomes answerable in terms of the Vision.
Injustice to the Vision becomes answerable in terms of the Flesh.

(AND ALL IN ACCORDANCE TO the terms and excises of Control (there is always the Heat/breathing, Barking!) &, conversely, to the disinclination from any Control (for there is also, as always, the Creature/breathing, Shrieking!)

Inevitabilities (if any): 1. Prescription of Freedom (exile, imprisonment, death), & Sickness (poverty, imprisonment, death.)

or 2. In Defeat & in Sickness life, existence, Being

can, and in most Natures does, blossom to a preciousness impossible to conceive at the beginnings of political and/or spiritual consciousness. (To Struggle & Be Doomed—Glory!)

or 3. History & Junk assume Control. (History "takes over"/Junk "takes over"—The Revolutionary & the Junky lose Control over Sword & Spike—become ambulatory deposits of Disloyalty & Deceit: the Ideal decayed/the Flesh woody/the Vision unremembered—"Wouldn't You?" Wm. B.)

or 4. Victory!—Success of the Revolution/Public Junk Enlightenment—Dictatorship of the Proletariat/Soma Opium Junk Paradise. (. . . with Always Danger of Corruption: Stalin Meglo-Creed disemboweling the Revolution/the Ever-Waiting OD Taste.)

II.

Argumentum

"Broadly speaking, the entire historical process is a re-fraction of the historical law through the accidental. In the language of biology, one might say that the historical law is realized through the natural selection of accident. On this foundation there develops the conscious human activity which subjects accidents to a process of artificial selection."

Leon Trotsky

"The purity of a revolution can last a fortnight. That is why the poet, the revolutionary of the soul, limits himself to the about-turns of the mind."

Jean Cocteau

III.

Conclusionem

There is a recognition and extension of Need from the lovely compulsion of our Creaturehoods of Sympathy and to Clarity—we would be Accurate and of Love within our Visions and our Histories. There is a Passion among us—the Planet breathing beneath us—there is a Length of Breath we share.

IV.

Ultimatus

The Purity of Revolution & the Purity of Junk . . . a haunt, Love.

16.

Yes, night *did* come in summers once. I speak now of seasons and of the interims. The thin brittleness of spring breathes life from a decaying winter, and so too fall molders winters under the rotten leaves of summer. Round and round old earth whirls and lucky it is we're not all spun off to clutter Space with our jangled bodies (bones rattling in our skin!) . . . the Void awash with shoes, hankies, hats, bits of cloth and old ceegar butts . . . the Whole Universe afloat with the domestic accessories of human life . . . the world empty of habitation and debris except for them creatures what live below the surface of earth: moles, worms, fishes, and such . . . the earth becoming a quiet place.

KIRBY DOYLE

17.

I lay on my guts in the big brass bed looking out over
the busted backyard. The man who had been painting his
red room had spit out the light and vanished and I wondered if his disappearance was in horror and disgust at
what he was doing . . .

It was early evening and lights were popping on in the
backs of all the buildings and I could see people shedding
their clothes as if they were tired and impatient with them.
Over to the right across the yard a floor below my watchment a lumbered man made weary gestures to a thin woman then settled back in a white chipped kitchen chair and
drank long swallows from a bottle of beer. Down farther
on the right a woman alone with forty years and orange
hair stood before a dresser mirror naked except for a gray
brassiere and sucked her rounded flap of belly in toward
her backbone with little grunts and smiles of imagined
success . . . Puerto Rican mothers oozed into exhausted
sleep before shouting television sets . . . all over stud-

102

ding the scabby backs of the buildings through windows nailed shut all the frigid winter long, murky tubes and screens threw imaged shadows jerking and gesturing like a million raucous halos in the New York night.

Dolly lay beside me breathing in sleep, positioned the same as when I had crumbled off her; her legs clung wide at the sheets and drawn up just enough to allow the soles of her feet to push flat down on the bed with leveraged expectation, ready even in sleep to press back at me; even her relaxation containing a readiness to hunch and thrust. I watched her soften in the used and refracted light of the darkening city and felt the scrape of hinged, hissing and hated doors inside me open a minuscule blink of space to let for just a shaved instant that near forgotten anti-feminist cocksman loathing and disgust of woman slither its empirical hatred over me. Slam the bloody door! . . . Snap the Hateful lock! . . . that is, I leaned over into her heat and with my tongue I kissed her dry breasts, her neck, opening my mouth to suction the tapered ends of her breasts, my tongue circling the ambered breasted tips, held the nipple gently like a soft candy between my teeth, finding the soft bulged belly beneath the darkened navel with my face, her swollen thighs, the faint curled spade of her lust, the hairlike silk-sheathed wands, the lips of her cunt opened and rolled back from each other like a half breathing mouth, the faint perfused whisper of moisture, my rough tongue edged in the separation, sliding down the membraned jut of pelvis under it into the relenting pliability of her vagina, the flaccid corrugation of zealous sensation, the raving liquid estuary of her sex extending the laved portico of pinked and melted flesh, her cunt a crystalline and marshy grotto in which to hide the hunger of my tongue, her diaphanous fluids pulled in osmotic leakage through the membraned folation of her awakening thecal burn, pellucid flux of manna and vaginal sap glisten my lips, my broaded tongue, the challenged muscles arching in search and greed for her aphrodisian lymph, meconic serum and amorphic acid of carnality glutting insensate my sex-sotted sight; the vulvar wrappings curled wide about my mouth, my voluble speech scalding her walls, the faint hairs that mound her cunt crushed like a limpid fern under the heaving wave of my mouth, her wedge of pale hair gentle beneath my jaw. Her hips motioned cautiously and her finger touched over my face with swift inquiry . . . on what wave of energy was my exhaustion hidden? My balls ached as if they had swollen within a bag of hardened fur. Sighting up along her belly, over her flattened breasts, I could see her teeth biting out over the edge of her lower lip . . . white row waiting through the opening of her smile . . . her eyes gauging my own smile, watching my grin. A flippant laugh scuttled in my throat and with it her moisture dried then and stiffened on my skin. I wondered on her rapid preconscious dream and fought down the spikes of curiosity in my brain that questioned if in her sleep she had been gobbled by the sea.

((Me & The Sea . . . Woof Woof! I snuffled around on her snowy form like a hot hog after winter roots . . . Fingers! . . . Bow Wow! I reveal my true identity: Boris Clitoris, Doktor of Exploritus Orificium! ("Extraordinaire, mon docteur . . . a vous (votre?) doigt medius technique!") There are of course myriad arguments of methodology plunging into the obtuse with academic zeal, but with a wave of my middle finger I extinguish them all as obscurantist cant and cavil. In modern creative sexual prosecution the only formal necessity is the establishment of a theme; in this case: Oral Dalliance With A Cunt. The implementation and insurance of a successful performance depend wholly upon . . . Free Improvisation! It is no more possible to render Orgasmic Satisfaction by the rigid pursuit of an established procedure than it is to grow a penis from the top of the head (as desirable as this might be). Aside from theme and desire, the only prescribed necessity is equipment. A man with no fingers operates with a decided handicap, not to mention he who is tongueless, and if the explorist were also without a cock it would be absolutely requisite that he develop an extremely facile set of toes and nose (in which case "coming" could be executed by a vigorous blast of air up through the sinus passages), but I fear satisfaction would be limited (not to mention attendant pregnancies, i.e., the issuance of "snotty little bastards," etc.). So be it established that if Theme, Desire & equipment are in evidence, you are, as it were, On Your Own . . . or, in the words of Aleister Crowley, a complete and howling crank in every particular except the one under discussion, "To do as thou wilt, is the whole of the law."))

Dolly was the proud possessor of a remarkably elastic cunt, especially if the engagement was a particularly heated one (that is, when I was at my best). Not that her snatch could expand and swell to a point where I, as she has jokingly (I think) proposed, could jam my whole head into it, but certainly to the degree where I could comfortably (for both of us) lodge my lower jaw and still have room to let my tongue wander where it would (according to her testimony, the blazing sensitivity of the walls of her vagina were heightened to near-insanity if I had a two- or three-day growth of beard on my face, although I would hesitate to make a generalization out of this point, receiving as I have, from females less inclined to this variation, complaints to the effect, "Jesus Christ, you bastard, take it easy . . . you're scratch'n hell out'a me!" . . . sorry . . . glub glub . . .)

Sliding the fingers of both hands into her cunt, which by this time was as easy as sliding into a bathtub full of vaseline, I could, by pulling the lips away from each other even more than the mechanics of her vaginal excitement had already done (as if I were trying to invert it), stretch her snatch out to an expansion where I could fit it over my face from eyebrows to chin like a hot meaty mask, and were it only detachable I could have marched in the Halloween Parade. This also afforded an excellent view six or seven inches down into her convulsive cavern quivering and rippling with the quakes and implosions of a multiple orgasm that would increase in both number and violence to be ultimately seismographically unmeasurable ("Sirrah, I'll break your bones," to quote Mme. D'Arblay). When this seismic sexual phenomenon threatened to scatter her in bloody bits and pieces about the room (Nay! The City! The Universe! Eternity!) I slipped my forefinger into her ass and rammed it to the knuckle . . . O Good Ladies and Gentle Men, need I tell you that she came neigh unto shitting all over me? . . . indeed, rivering her vaginal fluids over me with such copious and oceanic abundance that if I held my own life cheap and wished thus to play it away, easily (O with what Mad Ease!) could I have drowned there between her slippery thighs awash with her own pourings of love.

And no need I say that t'would have been anti-climactic to fuck her? Could she have still stood the blast and discharge I held in my volcanic cock? Nay, I fear not, surely it would have been her end for that's where it would have come out . . . her asshole blown right out the window and clean across Lower Manhattan like an unidentified flying object dripping with jism . . . the populace panicked . . .

radars of the world a'quiver with her whistling sphincter
. . . Air Armadas alerted . . . vast armies on the march
. . . diplomatic accusations hurled along the Transatlantic
cable . . . the U.N. stirred to imflammation like an infected movement of international bowels . . . precipitation of
nuclear war . . . the fall of governments . . . Death Rays
melting entire populations . . . World Revolution . . .
ANARCHY! No no, it would never do . . . rather, she
stuffed my boisterous cock into her mouth and drank
the Theandric Juices distilled deep within the erect man-
ufactory of my body.

18.

Fuck me and feed me . . . ding dong . . . Goddamn what a merry-go-round! I sought to pacify her with a hot dog (Meat Sticks Burning in a Bun!) from Riker's but nothing would do but a meat pie at the Times Square Horn & Hardart's . . . wanted to watch the big Camel sigh, blowing smoke rings she said . . . I suppose I could have made something of that but what the hell, it was her shot and who am I to mess with it? Who Indeed?

Amazing how the sound of anatomy after the fact of fornication takes on a victorious deception. After a good fuck I always figure I've had enough to last me unto dotage . . . get virtuous as blazes even to the point of avoiding the sight of her nakedness. She of course picked up on this and rightly angered and disgusted with my steely hypocrisy would languish about in her skin poking her nudity into my focus murmuring little innocent infuriations of domestic familiarity: "Do you think I'm getting fat?" while glutting her otherwise nicely rounded belly as far as the sag and extension of muscles would allow or, "Do you think my breasts are too big?" (or "too small," depending upon the strenuousness of post-coital morality) thrusting them up into my tight sight with her cupped hands posing like a young whore from out of the pages of *Playboy* or *Girl Parade* or *Peep* or some such other anti-feminist skin-mag offering succor to the masturbation of satyrist fantasies.

Prance she would and tend to domestic trivialities nakedly . . . cook a full meal in the raw . . . breasts dangling over the bubbling spaghetti . . . the cruel lewdness of her pubic hairs level with the salad . . . while with a feigned tone of "modern liberality" she threw out maddening little comments: "I so think it's wonderful not wearing clothes . . . so free . . . let the air into every little pore . . . so much more natural, don't you think?" then turn and show me her buttocks as she bent to the bottom rack of the refrigerator seeking vegetables. Anything. Leaning out the window like an inmate of Maiden Lane peddling her wares: sweeping, deep-breathing exercises, flopping onto the bed with cigarettes, candy and a book; attempting to discuss our finances; anything as long as she could do it without clothes to mock and taunt my biblical brittleness.

And it worked. Always I would sputter out pharisaical righteousness: "Hie thyself woman and cover thy nakedness!" Then she would scream with accusative laughter and throw her legs high over her head so that her snatch gaped and her asshole made a mossy wink at me: "You lousy fake! You goddamn counterfeit cocksman! Practice what you preach, you bastard! Don't come snuffling around me with that snotty fuckstick looking for a convenient hole to drop your load and then expect to stop it up with a moral cork! Had your little slap and tickle, have you? Coughed up your daily ounce of jism and feel better for it, do you? Just as soon brush away the taste of twat and go on to the editorial page as if sex were something you took from your pocket and fiddled with whenever you get vague stirrings between your legs? Screw off with that chilly jazz, Buster!" Laughing fit to die all the while . . . thought for a minute she was going to pee all over the ceiling. Had to laugh myself, though. She was right. "Piss on your tight-ass inclinations!" she'd howl. "What'a those inclinations mean to me? Piss on 'em, I say!" At times I was a warty cocksucker and there's no help for that except a blast between the eyes.

"I sorrow," sez I.

"I accept your sorrow," she sez.

"I'm a shit!"

"No, not really . . . just a bit stupid at times."

"Allow me to efface myself."

"How?"

"Leap out the window?"

"It'd lead to official inquiry."

"Flush my head down the john?"

"Screw up the plumbing."

"Expose myself in the subway?"

"A waste."

"How then?"

"No need to, really."

"I insist."

"Well . . . in that case . . ."

"Anything!"

"Get on your knees and kiss my big toe." I do.

"Now the other."

I do again. "Anything else?"

"Improvise!" she says, coming on like Little Orphan Annie to her blank-eyed dog Sandy . . . Arf . . .

19.

We sit in Horn & Hardart's scarfing beef pie. The Automat . . . a real wild shot . . . playing the food machines . . . lay four bits on the tired looking gent in the cashier's cage and get a handful of dirty nickels . . . clunk clunk clunk push the button and plop! . . . out slides a beef pie . . . insane!

20.

We came uptown on the hidden tubes shut and rattled under the city, quaking through the night with smoke pouring from our eyes. In the last empty car of a D train we turn on . . . Dolly coming on rather paranoid as is her wont at odd times when she is making grass . . . her taking surreptitious sneaky silent tokes on the joint which never fails to break me up . . . har de har har.

"What's so fuck'n funny?" she gurgled, holding back the smoke so only the words hissed around her teeth.

"You," I said, wiping my eyes. "You smoking that joint like The Man was under the seat," I said, holding my own breath so that only my soundcords shook but my tongue didn't flap nor my lung-sacks pooch.

"Yuk it up, Jim, but it pays to be cool . . . the mutha-fuckas are all over the place."

We sat there taking quick tokes on the joint and get-ting a very groovy sound until that joint ain't nothing but a wee bit of a roach. Delightful getting stoned on the subway and watching the other trains slide by. If you're on a *local* the bastard keeps stopping about every nine blocks so that it seems as if you're always either starting up or slowing down; in either case the train is moving a lot slower than the express trains that come blazing through the night whoosh whoosh whoosh in a long yellow smear of rapid faces peering at you as it goes wailing by. But the finest bit is when another train going about the same speed but from another elevation comes easing down on its sloping tracks and glides along window to window with you so that you and some stranger in the car opposite are kept practically face to face for a bit until one of the trains either descends or rises up above your eyes. Some pretty weird shots can go down when you're whipping along through the tubes beside another train . . . you staring at some guy, he staring at you . . . it's a compulsion, you can't take your eyes off him, especially if it's a fine-looking chick. But insane things happen, like the time Dolly and I were making it downtown on a 7th Ave. local one night when another train comes dropping down along side of us. The last car of the other train was next to us and right across from where we were sitting sat a small happy-looking gent with his necktie jerked over under one ear and his mouth open. The car he was in was empty except for him and our car was empty except for Dolly and me. We traveled along for about a half-mile staring across at each other. Dolly said something about what a weird looking cat he was and I said yeah and smiled at him. He grinned back and nodded his head a couple of times very quickly, and then, just as his train began to slope up to another elevation of track (or ours down . . . you never know . . . the whole thing is optically very elusive), he stood up and faced us with a huge red hard-on poking out of his fly . . . I mean like gigantic . . . as thick as your wrist and as long as your forearm . . . the end of it flattened against the glass like a snotty-nosed kid pressing up to a bakery window. He leaned forward as if to give us a better look. "Muuutherrr! Will ya look 'ut 'at?" Dolly whispered. "Yeah," I said and almost fell on my nut. Just as his train started coasting up out of sight he grabbed it and, jerking it hard three or four times, come exploded all over the window, then with a little sad and tired smile on his face he gently fingered his limbering piece and, stuffing it back in his pants, gave us a happy little wave of goodbye as his train disappeared. Someday I suppose he'll be caught and put where the birds won't shit on him and then there'll be just that much less joy in the world.

This night, though, as we're making the trip uptown, I think I see the ghost of Lester Young get into our car at 23rd Street. As the train shuddered into the old dirty tiled station and the doors whooshed open a real funky looking light-skinned Negro about forty years with faint-tinted shades, a porkpie, a light brown double-breasted 1940's type suit and, floppy sports shirt buttoned at the

neck came ambling in, sat down on one of the side bench-
es just inside the doors and sat a very battered horn case
down next to him on the seat. The door eased up and the
rubber lips kissed gently, happy at the inclosure because
magic was happen'n then . . . Old Porkpie Rides Again!
. . . I am bug-eyed with the sureness of my vision. I ram
Dolly one in the ribs with my elbow to make her look.
"What's ya, Crazy?" she says, bugged that I intruded on
her trip. "Look," I whispered in a smoky voice. "It's Prez!"
She looks at him, then looks back at me . . . blank . . .
clunk. "You been smoking too much grass . . . it's seeped
into your brain holes," and turns to the window again. I
ram her another shot in the ribs. "Leave off that elbow,
goddamnit! You try'n to cave in my bones?" She was getting rather pissed.

"I tell you it's Lester!" I said getting more excited.

"You jab me with that elbow again and I'm going to
Lester you, so help me Christ!"

"Will you use your eyes and look!" Lester had picked
up on our commotion and was watching it go down.

"Wow, I'll tell you, Tully, you ought to lay off grass and
the juice for awhile. I'm beginning to get worried about
you."

OK. She puts me down with this bit but as the train
rattles along I can't help staring at the guy because I am
sure it is Him . . . me and the ghost of Lester Young smiling all over each other . . . he just sitting there with one

leg crossed over the other and floating that faint sad and easy smile back at me like we were all on a journey of light-years. I could hear old D. B. Blues tumbling through my head and taking me with sweet breathing fatalism up through the airy atmospheres to look down and see all the hard and terrible jive going across in the world . . . warm sounds calling out from the brown and muted corners (Mike Light urges, "GESTURE in the dark brown space behind the door"), "It is happen'n even though locked away by cruel folks." Don't ask him, "Why so sad Prez?" I won't tell you about it anymore because you don't believe me.

34th Street and the doors coldly open and the ghost of Lester Young gone.

* * *

Poem For The Subway
i'm off my beat, the doors close
hear it HITLER

absolve us
(snood

mysophene

John Wieners
Winter 1960
New York

* * *

We eat beef pie in the automat at Times Square.

118

21.

Boxed . . . hampered . . . chained . . . imprisoned by the improbability of food!

"Waaa's happening?" I glance up from my food (chemical torrents gushing through my innards, expanding my life) and twist in my chair to see Orick shuffling his feet behind me. Who? Orick. Orick? Yes, Orick. Impossible! Why impossible? Because I left him 8 months and 3000 miles away. Not so, there he stands behind you watching your greedy intake of food . . . he appears hungry, but for what it would be difficult to say. Orick, is it? So it is my frantic friend of drunken days . . . Orick with whom I've split many a bottle into myself weak and laughing . . . nay, howling at my helplessness. Orick to whom crazed women sprang as if he were a meaty magnet electrified with sex . . . unstable women with slippery emotions demanding he fuck them through his hatred. Orick who massages his plastic paranoia into daily replicas of himself to be left seated in lighted and curtained windows to confuse

the unwary femme. Orick the self-made psychic crimi-
nal, like Gide's Lafcadio, administering upon himself
little systems of punishment, *puntas*, slight razor slash-
es across the belly-skin and arms in disciplined chastise-
ment . . . the blade guided by the hungry jewels of the
intellect but not with the disinterested emotions of that
Lafcadio; with fervor but not the evil maniacal efface-
ment of Crowley's disciples . . . self-punishment inflicted
with system and cruelty, but yet still with the benevolent
social sympathy of a humanitarian hangman weeping at
"the human condition" as he trips the yawning trap of
mutilation and death . . . wandering the planet with the
death-mask pulled tight to the chin in expectation of the
ease and inevitability of his sin . . . each comfort turned
to a castigation . . . the unbearability of going unpunished
. . . sitting drunken before his fireplace and vaguely
watching his hand grind itself into the splintered hunks
and edges of a shattered wine glass . . . treating the slashed
hand with lighter fluid to plunge it into the fireplace and
then hold the flame-bleeding hand up before his face and
weep silently alone in his dark rooms at the sight of it . . .
stalking through his college years with a revolver tucked
in his belt and vowed upon exploding it into the guts of the
first human who sent edged words toward him . . . stran-
gling in classrooms of the Great Thoughts of Civilization
. . . terrorized by the aspect of his goaded violence ter-
minating the haughty intellect of some academic rooster

... the warm pressure of destruction urged and cuddled at the thought of crushing in the skull of undergraduate puppies vomiting Aristotelian idiocies with the facile ripeness and stench of a thousand rhetorical rectums ... queasy theorems oozing out of a mouthy asshole. (Voice in my head: "OK ... CUT THE SHIT MCSWINE!") All this about his murderous impulses; that is, after being discharged Section 8 out of the army he didn't want to be fucked with no more ... this *no more* becoming *not at all* for if you did he would take out his gun and shoot you deader than a popcorn fart. This whole gun thing getting (fortunately) so out of hand (mind?) where he must needs stay drunk or kooked-out on goofers day and night to where his despair finally drives him out into the bare brown California hills to howl like a maddened hound at the fruity moon and explode bullets into the black shapeless mounds of night and throw the goddamn gun after them and to hell with it all. And this reminds me of Kitty, Orick's great Lovely Love; the two of them flaying sex over themselves to leave their hot skin like rags fluttering to a lean wind ... gasping out strangled conversations ... thrusting books into each other's hands ... begging that the other sleep ... angrily watching the breath of the uneasy sleeper ... flushed and muttered estrangements ... hissing threats over a maniacal telephone ... he following her on the streets ... watching each other in store windows ... crawling right into her mouth to beg and die

on the stinking street and cry mutilated anger on each
of her sorrows . . . phoning me in the middle of one icy
winter afternoon to ask, "Have you any idea what Kitty's
doing right now?" and I, fearful of his hysteria and bewildered, answering, "No, what's she doing now?" and he,
like an over-intelligent schoolboy hot with the answer,
"Sucking my cock, you son of a bitch . . . goodbye." . . .
and later, in San Francisco, in my damp apartment (the
walls yellowing), the night Dolly walked out on me for
the fourth time, he and I sitting around a jug of sweet
sickening juice so far out of it we could not hit our collective ass with both hands . . . he, all of an instant! . . . having a vision unpromised by his frustration but offered to
tantalize . . . he, shocked white and croaking, "I see it! Her
Bush! Right in front of my eyes! Her goddamn Bush!"
. . . bug-eyed staring at Kitty's cunt hair imaged and floating before his face, reaching out for it, "Fingers go right
through the fucking thing. Can't you see it? Shit, course
you can't see it! Fuck'n fingers go right through the fuck'n
thing!" . . . we tipping the big jug over our shoulders like
mountain folk . . . telling me a quaint little tale! "Did I
ever tell you I couldn't bear to have that chick give me
head? Yeah, it's true. Had an absolute fear that she wanted
to bite it off . . . started shaking all over when I saw her
teeth slide down over the head of it" . . . har har? Woof
Woof . . . laugh so hard I thought I was about to shit my
pants . . . him mumbling, "S'true. S'true . . . Goddamnit!

I tell you s'true" . . . the telephone jangling . . . I answering, "New Bijou Cat House. You call, we ball . . . day or night, black or white!" . . . it being Dolly say'n she wants to come home . . . me feeling powerful and terrified . . . yeah, OK, make it . . . Orick turning to me as I sit down to the jug again, "Man, I just can't stand your love affairs . . . all this fuck'n forgiveness," still somewhat pissed because I fucked Dolly for the first time in his bed and left two big wet puddles of come smack in the middle of his clammy sheets as a token of my friendship and appreciation; we had vowed to share all. Yes, he even demanding to see the manuscripts of my wandering book before I sent it away, demanding almost as if I were his evil biographer . . . forcing me to repeat over and over again that the book is about me, not him, but unable to accept this somehow . . . Orick, motionless and full of screams, now comes a shuffling through the planet to an unannounced and automatic assignation in the midst of this great greasy city to murmur, "Waaa's happening?" in my ear. "I come near to sliding out o' my chair." "Well I'll be Jesus Christ himself!" I said. "Just where in hell did you come from?"

"Over there, by the window. I seen ya come in. Howdee doo, Dolly?" Dolly blinks back at him, reinforced in her long-held conviction that he travels about in some ghostly 5th or 6th dimension.

"I mean in New York! When'd'ja leave the Coast? How long you been here, for Christ sake?"

"Three days now."

"Well where in the hell have you been? Why didn't you come to the pad? Where you been staying? What you try'n to do, avoid me?"

"Ease up on the questions, Percy. Smile when you reach for your anger. If you're going to ask so many questions write 'em down . . . shiiit, ah' cain't a'member 'em all!" assuming an easy evasive come-on when trapped into directness.

"Well, where have you been hiding?"

"Ain't been hiding at all. Ah' been holed-up with Jarry O'Rooney in that spooky loft of his down on Broadway just off Ninth Street. Sure is some weird shit go'n down in that loft. Absolutely gigantic! Tells me there's parts of it he's never been in, room after room, hidden staircases and secret panels. Stretches for a whole city block. A body could get lost in that big old place . . . about half of it been took over by a whole passel o' junkies . . . terrible scene . . . looks like a shoot'n gallery . . . ya never seen so many spikes in yer life. But it ain't the junk what makes it all so spooky, it's the magic and mumbled signs and such what's go'n on. Them junkheads is all down there come'n on like they was disciples o'th Great Beast or some'th'n . . . down there shoot'n up and perform'n magic rites with much wave'n of arms and genitals. Why just last night Jarry comes home to find his paintings all slashed up and three years worth of poems ain't nothing now but a heap of gray ashes laying admidst the scattered garbage and ref use of his unkept domicile. Comes home as I say and finds his room and things all tore up and right smack in the middle of the whole rupped-up mess there's this terrible look'n junky cold out on the floor stark-ass naked wif a big chalk circle drawed around him and bits o' colored glass and little bitty stubs o' candles burn'n about the edge of this chalk circle and clasped in his hand on his chest is a great big mutha'fucka of a gleam'n knife and so Jarry figures he ain't to be fuck'd with considering as how this fella must have some terrible spiritual problems, so he works it out as how he ought to split and leave them old cold rooms to the junkies . . . says it ain't the magic and the strange carry'n on what spooks him, but that parade of junkheads is sure to bring on the heat and he has no eyes to get busted . . . figured he was right so I evacuated right along with him . . . we both out on the street now . . . ain't seen him since morning . . . said he was going to scuffle up a place so's we can fall out . . . was supposed to meet me here at eight, but I don't think he completely grasps the mechanics of time." He glanced around the automat with a great indifference.

"OK, fine, but why didn't you come to the pad? You got the address . . . it's only a few blocks away from Jarry's place. You been avoiding me? What the fuck! I haven't seen you in months and when you do drag your ass across the hinterlands you come on like Sam The Turkey!" forgetting, of course, that I hadn't been there myself until last night . . . most uncool of me, feeling slighted . . . suppose to just let it happen and all this. Very nasty of me coming on betray'd.

"Now don't get shook, Percy. I didn't come around because I just couldn't bear the sight of you standing at the door'o'yo domicile an' coming on like a householder with The Big Hello . . . make me feel like a damn barbarian come snuffl'n down out'a the hills to stir up some shit." All this with a friendly smile at Dolly who he always figured rather loathed him. She really didn't, but my relationship with him was always somewhat suspect . . . full of hidden deficiencies, subtle sympathies of an anti-feminist cast, the mostly imagined tug of loyalties between The Friend and The Mistress leaving The Kid standing in between in a tattered state of confusion . . . etc., *ad nauseam.*

"I just figured we'd wander into each other on the street, let it happen, you know?"

"Yeah, I guess." I felt bugged by his continental indifference. Dolly was amused, silently bemused.

"Drove clean across country with Roz and the cat she's gonna marry, name of Leigh . . . reckon she's about to marry him a'count of she being knocked-up . . . least she thinks she is, knocked-up that is."

"That must have been a cozy trip," Dolly slyly (she thought) suggested.

"Sort'a. I had to do most of the driving . . . they was fuck'n in the backseat damn near all the way across the nation. I got real horny watch'n 'em in the rear-view mirror . . . almost demanded a fuck for the driver just so's he could keep his eyes on the road. Shouldn't complain though, I guess, didn't get a taste but didn't have to pay for no gas and oil neither."

"Where did they go?"

"Damned if I know! We come through the tunnel that lies under yonder river, hit the tall buildings on t'other side and I yells, 'This is it! We're here . . . lemme out!' Last I saw of them, they was being sucked into a traffic jam. Not me though! I just zipped down the street all agog with the frenzy of it all." With a gracious wave of his arm he directed my gaze out the plate-glass window into the electric madness of Times Square. "Hot Damn! There ain't nothing like that out in the provinces!"

Bedazzled by lights and gaudy motions! My emotions and concepts of attachments are as excessive as my language. Such self shitty pity! Who don't I suspect? Watching Orick calmly enthuse I wondered if it is possible to die without knowing who we've betrayed.

I am struck with that which Albion Moonlight has observed: "There was never a better friend, we say, and we mean: He never bothered me, nor I him."

22.

We sat and shucked, the Automat murmuring about us.

* * *

A bearded blur in the door . . . a shabby greatcoat flapping in the moist air. I look up hard to focus and behold the late belated Jarry O'Rooney rushing, counting his excitements on the eternal calendar of his mind.

"Jarreeno! What's happen'n baby?"

He alights at the table like a haired and flustered Prophetic Bird bursting with messages.

"Hey hey hey hey HEY! That Sonny Rollins is some great big fat pelican! I mean his scoobeedoo! I mean like I been hear'n his scoobeedoo!"

"Where baby?" Dolly asks, for she really loves this feathered boy.

"All over, Lovely, all over! Like down on the East Side I seen him lean'n on a streetcorner watching the sunshine, and I says to him, 'What's Happen'n Sonny?' and he says to me, 'The Sunshine, Man, the Sunshine' . . . and it was . . . He Knows!"

"Crazy," Pooh Bear sez, "but did you find us a flop?"

"Not so, Fatso . . . not so, but we have been invited to a party. Want'a make it?" he says, turning to Dolly and me.

"Where's the party going to be, Sweet Stuff?" Dolly again. Sometimes I wonder about her and him. She says it's a Mother Thing, he being only 19 and out loose by his self with no one to watch after his feeding habits, but still I do get anxious at odd moments and somewhat filled with suspicious notions.

"At Miss Kids'. She's gonna have a psychic breakdown and wants everyone to come watch. It's her biannual flip and a graduate research team from Sara Lawrence is going to be there collecting data on her speciality. If nothing else we'll at least get a strange lay. Besides, I hear that the Black Pansy Mob will probably be there with a suitcase full of Scoobeedoo . . . OOPAPADA REEEVOUT!" he sings out with as is his wont when peepin' from the pockets o'joy. I myself even feel the nebulous beginnings of a hard-on.

"Lovelorn ladies and licentious libations dragging libidinous hooks of memory through my hair . . . "Orick it seems was pleased by the possibility of plenitudinous profligation (. . . it also seems that I am getting ridiculous) . . .

Wait! Let me say that I feel a vague and pushing necessity for the telling of lies; that is, I must sneak my words between my teeth . . . (the first axiom of Tully McSwine's Theorem of irresistible Horseshit: "Barely open yer lips.") . . . Hello there, this is Tully talk'n . . . I am in control here (and the orange and black ladybug what lives amongst the iron innards of my writing machine is hard put to it to keep from being mashed into a glob of glue as I recklessly hammer on) so do not get cute and ask for explanations; if I can I will, or rather, if I can *and have seen it upon the planet*, I will. A question of ethics, in a weird way. That is, if I take a sudden notion to talk about the aspect of Rudy Vallee I will do so whether the Cabbage-Sellers (as the Leonic Ogre so calls the 20th c. counterpart of the Hamiltonian "Great Beast" of, by now, lobotomized democracy; to quote the L.O., "Other than the artist, all those who creep about the planet perform only two functions; that is, as spreaders of genes—in hopes that in accordance with the law of averages that in any prescribed ocean of come over a generation the birth of probably not more than ten artists may therein swim, thereby maintaining the image of Man in some approximation to the idea of intelligent life—and as sellers of cabbages. After all, we have to eat.") find it palatable or not. That is, what a Cabbage-Seller finds palatable is not my problem, is the Cabbage-Seller's, and so whether or not Rudy Vallee can be swallowed either whole or in part is no concern of mine . . . I can only serve him up and season him to my own taste, and so the problem of how to eat Rudy Vallee becomes *just* your problem, not mine, and so (again) if you can't get him down please do not noise it about in my direction for if ever I should meet you at an unfortunate literary gangbang of malicious snicker snack do not come ah-h-hemming up to me with yer coy or gouty pronouncements upon my abilities as a pornographic digressionist or else yer liable to get a punch right in the fuck'n head. Let us put it this way, if you've gotten this far in my (what? tale? OK . . .) tale and your asshole is getting all tightened with indignation at my: 1. bad and "undisciplined" writing, 2. messy morals, 3. lack of political stance (take note of the nearly complete diffusion of politics inherent in this welcoming direction . . . I really mean perhaps the absolute hopelessness of stance or the impossibility of the historical gestures, i.e.: war, revolution, social legislation of enlightened bent, martyrdom (pick your own cross), pacifist protest (rife with internally syntactical contradiction), ex-YCL horsey intelligentsia all as humorlessly ugly as some Standard Oil or United Fruit toady starving Arab or Guatemalan children . . . do not tell me that millions go hungry while I can still peep from the deep curtained windows of my cave and see that the whole fuck'n world is starving, stuffed to the eyeballs at the banquet table of lies and fear . . . skin caving in around our bones and brains as we sit gorged and grunting from glutted meals of hysteria) or 4. corruption, then know ye this: 1. I know nothing of "good," "bad" or "discipline," but know only that the art of writing for me involves no less than *giving an accurate Voice to my Vision of the planet*, and if my Vision is that the planet is "bad" than that Voice shall be "bad," but nothing as simple-minded as this is involved here, for the planet is neither good nor bad nor disciplined nor is it spinning along in heroic couplets nor in any other diagram of precise geometric verbiage as would the Deaf & Sightless Penny-Poets & Politicians have us believe . . . rather, the planet operates on its own flux and flow of rhythms and motions and it is my job as a writer to understand and be accurate to them. 2. I believe only in the morality of life (which involves cunts and cocks and loyalties and friendships and vast chasmic depressions and cool fags and just about everything that isn't a lie or dead). All other systems of morality being no more than expediences for everyone to devour everyone else. I am a very moral man . . . my morality is strenuous, I struggle with it in my dreams. I believe that which Patchen says, ". . . I hate their heaven, I could invent fifty better ones in a single day." 3. Politics carries the stench of death. Fidel Castro is the only politician within my memory who has any intention of keeping his campaign promises, and consequently, is violently hated by all other politicians because of it. Whenever in doubt about politics and politicians just remember who are the minters of money and the payers of police. 4. The corruption of writers is twofold in both Voice and Vision; that is, Corruption is to give active lies to the Voice and/or to relinquish the Vision (or to deny it altogether). Most of American poetry and damn near all American prose is completely without Vision and nothing but a well-paid pack of Lies! With great liberality I believe I could count the uncorrupt poets and prose writers who are still alive in this country on my fingers and toes, of which digits I have twenty. Self-imitation is probably the most popular bed of corruption in which the writer may lie. This disease particularly effects old writers (Wordsworth and Hemingway in their dotage are simple-minded and obvious examples of this corruption becoming, as they did, parodies of themselves), perhaps because as their hearts become drier so too does their well of Vision. Of course the greatest number of writers are those who were absolutely poverty stricken of Vision long before they ever put finger one to a writing machine and who must needs climb aboard someone else's hobby-horse.

Corruption? Yes, but the Other too!

This, my generation, has picked up a language left wincing and atrophied from the polite fright, scaley metrics and antique preciousness of our literary forebears and in Honest Bravery has Voiced Horrific Nerved & Beauty of Mind Electric UP FRONT WITH LUNGS FULL WITH EYES AND THE TONGUE IN SEVEN

DIRECTIONS WITHIN THE HEAD TWISTING TO
SAY FOUNDERING AND JOYFUL ILLUMINATION
OF DISCOVERIES OF THAT WHICH IS BEFORE THE
EYE!

The bravery of my generation is mark'd more solid
and rapid than any since the Jutes and Danes slaugh-
tered South Scandinavian dragons in the beginning of
our tongue . . . the Sightings of Blake and such Melvillian
heroism returning to the language: Dr. Sax, Naked Lunch,
Maximus, all Endyten & Doomed (inspiration brighter
than the glow in Hamlet's skull), to be pinched and picked
and pissed upon by cabbage-selling fingers expecting
fear . . . McClure's Clear & Might Document of FUCK
in Purgation & Cleansing of the Moral Sores and Pox
meanminded civilizations of cynicism have infected and
inoculated (Cancer perpetuating Cancer bred to Inherit-
ed and Congenital Sickness and Fear) into word-worried
and bounded ligaments of Spirit Meat Tongue Flesh Fuck
of pre-born uncensor'd Intellect & Body—Man & Woman
Skin Pouring Together . . . The Lordly And Isolate Satyrs/
The Great Bear Man . . . and Fine Jack Wieners (I do not
dwell on his suffering) incapably caught in the balance
of Man Lover'd offered Sex to his Old Man Blond Lover
Man that populations drunken with stupidity would
trample . . . Peter O. (his dusty finger aloft to his nose with
Kindness More Noble than all the tricky postures of that
old feared and word-warty sophist numbing at the toes as

his last thought belied the Human Meat & Intellect with
more finality, thoroughness and disinterest than a lifetime
of Ugly Headed arguments and wordy gymnastics) Good
Peter O. baking whole fish in milk and the scent of bay
leaves to offer his gentle brother and his Lover (He, Nasty
& Eye Gleam, this Beloved, Uneasy Learned, his boiling
tongue swollen in his Mouth, his casted skein (Galilee
Fisher?) of Hurt, for Open & Young I long ago at him re-
spect proffered and he would to accept and painfully spit
back as he moved behind the security of my unprotected
brain . . . somehow safe behind my dangerous ignorance
of my own sex ((do I imagine all this? spin up fictions to
adjust the mind to the body's ignorance?)) . . . he frightened in his real greatness to the cloying tricks of The Street
(The City!) but mine own, yet a mountainous shadow of
kindness ((but not here the Image, and even less the re-
ciprocal pleasure of brutal substance)) barely leaked into
my glaring and squinty ignorance . . . in an epistle to Mike
Light (this brilliance of selected confidant) ". . . how can I
return them to him?" . . . this when my globe was newly
on the mend and I shaky with experience . . . but no, fur-
ther, past the irritations of a minor itch . . . this the creep
of Accursed Blindness after Sighting the Planet & All Its
Rhythms (like Milton perhaps, easily clutching prizes of
lament upon the occasioned memory of a friend's death)
and then ever after, yearly implosions of the same blindness telescoping the Vision outward past the collapsing

Sight of fearful human love . . . worrying this blindness
. . . running his hands over it . . . his filthy hands just
lifted from his crotch . . . not sure of his lack of sight . . .
feeling for it . . . discarding it blank and unseeing . . . his
seminal juices still hot to his hand and running the tears
to madness in his stretched and whitened eyes . . . bleary
films of apocalyptic stance and gesture . . . of the intellect
and the nervous motives of the body cast over and past
the eastward curve of the earth . . . knowing time from
the direction of the sun's rise . . . He/Unchaste Apocalypse
breathing the stench'd Planet's eons of gathered Wisdoms
& Wickedness! . . . this lampless Aladdin wearing the
garments of Joyful Poverty creeping with excited words
like the licey itch of stout àBecket's welcoming shirt of
hair . . . this Cathedral of my generation for whom Good
Peter O. bakes fish in milk and scent of bay leaves . . .

* * *

Now here I swell on Bravery & Corruption . . . have I
yet said aught of either?

If you stalk through the planet with eyes glaring,
then much can be made of the hurted hundreds of men.

I was concerned with the Cabbage-Sellers: to accept
this blather of "spreaders of genes" and "sellers of cabbage" demands a pocketing of oneself in extreme isola-

tion (a superior isolation I might add) of which cynicism is a very probable direction, which cynicism being in direct antithesis of any morality of life. Yea, now Cabbage-Sellers there are (mostly) and in advanced moments of bitter stance (the world rapidly churning to shit) these folk appear to assume a third function; that is, as war-makers. The proclaimed and insisted purpose in the "spreading of genes," "selling of cabbage," and in the "making of war" is the "advancement of civilization," and as the gene spreading, cabbage-selling war-makers are all civilized people, so civilization answers its approval with a nod . . . a nod . . . a nod . . . a nod. Butchers and brokers dealing in the statistics of death . . . death compounded in profit rise . . . steely stocks of morality traded on the markets of hysteria . . . blind rectal lips of civilization straining to disgorge its meal of murder. 'Tis the onus of the anus: *"Ooze on, ye buttered fellows, ooze on!"* Insufferable, isn't it? Unsubtly subtle . . . the corruption of the civilized, like those three dots . . . a backdrop type of make-believe agony and silences, unhappy enigmas, unplumbed profundities distracting the attention while the creep of words leak out of speech undetected. Yet, from far beneath the chill of my own purity I am vaguely aware of compassion. Here: my gene-spreading, cabbage-selling vagabond uncle Charlie who all through his short life was affixed with the doomed nickname of "Gloomy." This Uncle Gloom (as he was patronizingly called by all his relatives, including me . . . I who loved him more than most) moved slowly and sadly through life like a cliff of snow quietly melting. The god my Uncle Gloom silently believed in exampled him in life as failure, in fact failure in all except death. His doom seemed anal centered; that is, the relatives in their energetic eagerness ascribed the beginnings of his failure to either one of two incidents. The first was when at the age of 7 or 8 he and my father were playing "Stab The Hun," a game in which they would throw mushmelons into the air and give them an under-handed stab with a clasp-knife as they came down. It just so happens that as my father, who was around 11 or 12 at the time, was coming up with his knife to meet a descending "Hun" my Uncle Gloom was bending over to pick up another melon and caught my daddy's blade full in the ass, from which wound he came damn near to dying of tetanus. From that time forward I think there was formed in his gentle mind the suspicion that my father by either financial success or bodily assault was out to get him. This is most grievous and unfortunate because periodically throughout his life he found it necessary to seek out my father and lean full-weight upon his stern strength. His shame must have been torturous.

The other incident, which was spoken about by my father with a bitterness generally foreign to him, took place in the early '30s when the Depression had been turned up full volume and the whole world had gone piss poor. My

Uncle Gloomy, who at the time was around 17 years old, was making his way afoot up through the San Joaquin Valley headed, I believe, toward San Francisco. To keep himself in grub and a few pennies he'd managed to pick up a day's work here and there cutting grapes or digging post-holes or some other such transient work what was to be found on the dusty failing farms of those foreclosed years. One beautiful sun-blasted afternoon he was hiking along a hot back road outside one of those dozens of baked and insignificant little shit-station farm towns like Ceres or Hickman or Crow's Landing or Volta or Tranquility or Pixley or Hub when down this damn road came speeding a dirty battered Ford Sedan that slid to a stop across the road when it got up to him. Two huge meaty cops leaned out of the car with their pistols pointed at my uncle's head. "This son-of-a-bitch'll do!" shouts one big purple-faced bastard who's gut dripped down over his gun-belt. Before my uncle could collect himself enough to inquire into the nature of their agitation, the one who shouted ups and bashes my Uncle Gloomy a terrible blow upside the head with the barrel of his revolver. Down goes my uncle, dropping to the dust with a four inch rip across the side of his head and lay there dazed and bleeding like a hammered calf. The other cop, not content with the insensibility rendered my uncle by the smash on the skull, lays on a couple of swift ones in the ribs with his trooper boots, then they grab him like he was a limpid sack of shit, drag him across the road and slam him in the back of the Ford. He wakes up in some dank and fetid jail cell to find himself accused of armed robbery to which charge his captors demand he sign a confession. This he refuses to do, having never stolen a blessed thing in his innocent life. Now this round-faced naive right-off-the-farm uncle of mine would no more commit robbery, even in those hungry times, than he would piss in the holywater font of St. Patrick's Cathedral. With great politeness, a politeness that only the very gentle seem honestly capable of, he explains who he is, where he came from, where he's going and why, which explanation is met with even more brutal beating during which his right ear is almost torn from his head and one eye completely closed, the effect of which was to leave a tendency of that eyelid to droop for the remainder of his life, thereby adding to the ever-increasing aura of gloom that hovered about him. Again he refuses to sign the confession simply, I suppose, because he had not robbed anyone. It must have slowly seeped into the crab-like brains of the Heat that the beatings weren't getting them very far, so they stripped his clothes from him and tied him face-down and spread-eagled on a low, wide wooden bench, then stoked a fire in an old coal-stove in which fire they heated the business-end of a poker. When they figured it was hot enough one of them sat straddled on my uncle's back and held the cheeks of his ass apart while the other slowly and without too much success tried to jam the hot poker into his rectum. I doubt very much whether more than two or three inches of glowing iron poker actually got into his ass, but nonetheless pretty much of a mess ensued. Not a very imaginative torture but a painful one and one that is pretty obviously illustrative of the particular sexual-psychotic bent of those good police officers. Instead of confessing, as these two worthies had every reason to expect (a confession that would have very readily been delivered up if they had been so tormented), my uncle merely responded by passing out. This quaint, albeit medieval, little system of criminology apparently went on for some time to where it must have become overbearingly obvious to even the numbed sensibilities of these two agents of justice that instead of a confession they were liable to end up with a corpse to which was attached an unexplainably scorched sphincter. They dragged his clothes back onto him and, throwing his body (about which there was probably a great question as to the state or degree of life) back into the car and driving an undetermined number of miles away from the town in which they had committed their brutality upon my uncle, they dumped him out on a deserted road where the next morning he was found by a truck-farmer heading towards Oakland to sell his load of cabbages. In Oakland he was hospitalized for some weeks and so terrorized was he by this outrage that it was not until months after that my father was able to pry the most reluctant and barest out-

lines of the sorty from him. As such things go I am sure
that it was just a minor horror in the work-a-day world
of the police in this country and if the realization arrived
that a refinement of methodology was needed I have no
doubt that the two sadists who butchered up my uncle are
by now respected Sultans, Chiefs and Pootaabs of Police
in some decaying shitsville suburb of America. Efficiency
in the form of roasted rectums is rewarded in the police
business. In later years, I have become convinced that I
personally have, among the nobles of the San Francisco
Police Department, come into immediate contact with
the direct descendants of my Uncle Gloomy's goonish
torturers; having not yet had a burning poker shoved up
my ass, but still having been the recipient of a couple of
minor beatings, I know to some extent whereof I speak.
The back elevator of the San Francisco City Prison is in-
famously notorious for mechanical failures and stoppages
between floors where the mentally defective Heat of that
fair city may take their pleasures upon whatever prisoners
they might have in hand; a sort of municipally sponsored
sadism of which this ultracivilized country of ours seems
so fond. The police of New York are, I have been led to
believe, thieves and cowards. The police of Berkeley must
be enriched of a college degree to be ordained in the
smashing of heads. Los Angeles has the highest incidence
of out-and-out murderous psychotics on its police force
of any major city in the USA. But San Francisco cannot be

out-done for the righteous viciousness of its police. This is accomplished by screening out those applicants who show the most minute glitter of intelligence, and selecting only the stupidest thugs, goons and mugs the city can disgorge from its social bowels. We are a nation of police, rapidly becoming a police-state, and every stroke of our education from the schools and academies right through the huge and blatant social horns of mass entertainment pump to insulate our emotions and numb our sensibilities into indifference toward the steady smothering of our civil liberties and freedoms by the police and the politicians. They are winning. In terms of my own lifespan I look for the congressional introduction and acceptance of a constitutional amendment suspending the Constitution itself altogether . . . and then what will protect us from the police?

*   *   *

To hell with that, I was speaking of my Uncle Charlie, called Gloomy by those he loved. Reviewing his life it seems to me that his few years on the planet were spent in catching hot pokers in the ass, or the ear, or the eye, and that finally he'd just had enough and to hell with it all. Failure, both by way of the money system and the neural system, seemed to leak from his pores. Eventually he collapsed into a hospital with what was called in those days "a nervous breakdown"; in short, he appeared to be on the verge of flipping out of it altogether. I don't know what went on down in that stinking hospital but the professionals must have done their usual grim practices of jamming electric spikes in his head or sawing off a hunk of brain because when my father brought him (along with his wife and baby son) home to live with us there was a sure death moving slowly through him; I could see it in the strained flesh of his mechanical smile; death's shift propelling his hands constantly creeping over the arms of his chair; death sagging his whole body and hiding his pale blue eyes behind a dull unseeing translucent film; death easing the sound of his words out of his speech undetected.

The house we lived in stood four stories and sunny captured in a lush wild two-acre garden of jungle high on the Sausalito hills that hovered over the Bay. French windows and fine old walnut piano and crackly fireplace and stairs leading everywhere to half-landings and breakfast nooks. On sun-streaming days I could sit quietly in deep-scented sofas and watch the galaxies of dust spiral in the soft shafts of sunshine. A fat and fixed tiger cat shadowed itself through the green grounds trapping the house, battering its way through butterflies. The top floor was my wall-window room from which I spied the cities and the bays and the boats. French doors here too led to a baked sunporch high above the green garden and the sunken stone lily-spattered goldfish pond.

On silent Saturday afternoons when family had disappeared into weekend society I would hours wander my
own brown-shingled high house and graciously touch the
dust and sunbeams that floated the rooms; sipping my
father's Hennessy from a large and fragile brandy snifter
as I entertained my own ghosty self from room to den to
library commenting upon the acquisition of a fine del
Sarto Annunciation hanging upon a nude wall of the
study, or gently fondling the lithe bronze Perseus attrib-
uted to Cellini and bequeathed down through my six-
hundred-year-old family; the jade-streaked Chinese vase
ushered up to my protection from some antique dynasty
would receive a faint stroke from my pale hands as I made
my way to the piano to lightly finger Chopin etudes in the
dying dusk. In a far corner Mad Jack would sigh upon
the quietude of the globe and holding his busied brain
in his hands examine it for any stray distressing leak of
half-masked ideas while The Man In The Bright Nightgown warmed the chilly lobes of his ears before the cavern place blaze of spark bursting logs. Kid Sorrow alone
paced the upper floors. Upon night the gas lamps would
be lit and settling myself in my dolorous oak-carved and
panelled study I would snuffle just an absolving pinch of
cocaine from a chalice wrought and hammered in the ancient wastes of Byzantium to clear my head, then plunge
into alchemic folios that crumbled with archaic secrets
beneath my very fingertips while Galli-Curci wheezed

from the gramophone. It is in these surroundings that I allowed my Uncle Gloomy to die, for I could not bear to watch death daily move toward him unprotested.

One Friday mid-morning as the bright air stood motionless in the trees outside, my uncle heavily climbed the narrow stairs to my high-windowed bedroom in which my Shetland purebred drowsed upon my bed with his blue eye open, locked the door behind him and cast about through the brilliance of the day that had filtered into the room. My bone-handled hunting knife lay across my desk, and in long unhesitant motion he raised it up high over his head and brought it swiftly down into his intestines. I am sure he saw the spray of his own blood that sent my Shetland hunched and whining to the far corner of the room. His whines aroused three of the family who were taking a leisurely breakfast below. My uncle's wife left the table and, following the terror of my dog's whine up the stairs, arrived outside my locked door. She called out and my uncle told her to go away. Fingering her panic she fled downstairs, screaming for her brother Bill who bounded up and without stopping went completely through my locked bedroom door just in time to see my uncle going over the sunporch outside the French doors to fall stabbed and broken into the sunken stone lily-and-blood-spattered goldfish pond where he died blinking in the bright morning sunlight.

146

* * *

Why am I telling you this about my uncle here in the midst of a Voicing upon one day's journey in the Great Greasy City, time and space so terribly removed from it all: a good fourteen years after the fact and in round numbers about 3000 miles from the point of impact of my uncle's body and vastly unknown miles in those 14 years zig-zagged from the Ryukyuian edge of the East China Sea to the rigid winter barrenness of Madhouse Medfield Massachusetts where I went to visit Mad Jack, toothless and planetary under the confinement of his mother's hysteria? Wait . . . let me leap over the parenthetical thing in search of clarity . . . the question: What has Uncle Gloomy's business to do with a day in the life of the T. McSwines? Wait. It dimly has to do with civilization, of which I think I have had quite enough. This thing, this thing about civilization . . . I think the most unfortunate . . . whaaaaaaaaat? I think? I think I . . . think I think . . . I think think . . . think think think . . . I I think . . . think think I . . . think I I . . . IIIEEEYYYAAA think Thank THUNK!

Please follow!:

What I am using-doing-trying-composing upon this strangled alphabet of mine own invention is test the tick-

ing devises of terrorism of which I think it best that nothing be said at the present other than here's a neat little
bomb to be set a'shuddering in yer morning mush, my
mossy dears: *I have been captured by my brain and am
being held as an unwanted prize.* Clear enough, that.

While I was doing time in The Academy I was made to
feel and concede the Game to the triple forces of civilization, intellectuality and liberalism, and so consequently
was working hard to perfect myself in the stance of the
Civilized & Liberal Intellectual, or maybe it was the Intellectual and Civilized Liberal & or then again it might
have been the Liberal Intelligent Civilized, anyway, something like that (the 3 phyla not of necessity being mutually
compatible) and found that in the five worried years of
that unhappy and near-fatal trip as I tediously construct-
ed and fitted together all the available tinker-toys of
Human Enlightenment (for which I duly received a most
pretty document) that fell within the scope of My Particular Field (Unglish Literature I believe t'was) I would
periodically come apart like a soggy jigsaw puzzle and sit
through four classes a day for weeks like a malfunction-
ing zombie staring in utter disbelief as my professorial
keepers droned on, splintering ambiguities like a squad
of tweedy cyclotrons peeling the atom of knowledge. My
hair would grow long and my underwear dank. My ball-
point pen would droop in my hand like a limp dick. After
an hour's exposure I would find that I had filled twelve

notebook pages with such as, ". . . the oblivious influenc-
es of the Industrial Outhouse upon the minor workings
of the Major Workers becomes increasingly decreasing as
is seen and unsteadily noticed among the hidden spon-
dees in the unpublished shouts of such principal figures
as Blind Alf and Montejoy Lovebody . . ." etc. etc. glab
glab. At the culmination of years of zealous literary schol-
arship, unending clockticks of search through hundreds
of bins full of pigs, bones and polite miles of intimate
yet restrained closeting with one's Masters Advisor over
deftly tapped cigarettes and seas of piss-colored tea I was
definitely prepared to state that "The Eve Of St. Agnes"
was without doubt, no doubt at all, written in iambic
pentameter. I had fuck'n well arrived, Jack! If you've ever
been groped by a caved-in and yellowish dean of graduate
study you'll know what I mean.

Nothing can stop the leak of time, and so with this un-
haltable seepage of seconds, minutes, hours, days, weeks,
months, years, generations, decades, centuries and infinite vastliness of space and motion the Physiks of the
Planet are slowly recognized and with Recognition comes
the pretense of Understanding from whence comes Control from whence comes the possibilities of Power from
whence comes Avarice from whence comes Exploitation
(do you see the bone of this word? . . . that structural part
which holds it together? . . . that tempered tube of calci-
um in which is prison'd the taste and flavor of idea? Look

in the middle of packed and oiled letters . . do you find
". . . ploi . . ."? and this "ploi" from Old French to the Middle English turns to "ploy" . . . and what is *ploy*? . . . its
aspect mirrored and exposed in its linguistic personality?
. . . its personal and secret countenance? Ploy is *Trick!*
Inside our social activity we manipulate the ploy of man-
ners and moralities to such a degree of refinement that
we must needs ploy the ploy; ie: "Do you solemnly swear
(!) to tell the truth (!!), the whole truth (!!!), and nothing but the truth (!!!!) so help you God? (!!!!!)" . . . (the
whole general ploy encasing at least 5 traditional ploys)
. . . and the answer: "I do." Ha Ha Clang!!!!!! . . . THE
PLOY PLOYED! Nimsovich must have studied the
Philosophy of Legal & Moral Refinements from all
Learned and Intuitive Positions before he ignited his rev-
olutions of chess, by which I mean that Nimsovich must
have watched the social gestures of humankind with icy
eyes, his unsympathetic brain stripped of both pity and
cynicism like a lean and inexhaustible spider watching
the spastic hysteria of a fat and clumsy bug flapping in
the web of adhesive fate. We look down into our word
and find it cuddling tricks between the "Ex . . ." and the
". . . tation" of its respectable extremities; these polite
devices of verbiage which by the prefixual and suffixual
signals give out fumes of dimension, pretending a clarity of direction they do not possess. Pay them no mind,
but watch them, for they mislead the intellect around and

around the idea-bone of the *word* and never allow it to be directly fingered nor sucked upon. If ever a man offers to "Employ" you—BEWARE!) . . . I was saying, from whence (from Avarice) comes Exploitation, this all in turn offering infinite opportunity for the Original Syphilis of Professionalism ("We, the Wise & Learned, profess . . .") to spread its malignant and impacted growth unchecked, for the death of one human fear contains within it the birth of another. As the slivered needle is held floating and captive within the compass and forced by unreasoned energy to swing about always to one and only One Direction, so too the brain of man arrows to one point unregardful of his frenzied jerks and dancing. Man navigates upon the guide of Static Fear.

God may change his aspect (or we may do it for him) from that of Wrath to that of Forgiveness, and so too our mouth-twisting Fear of God softens into a moist-eyed Love of God, and as the immediacy of a Man Imaged and Loving Christ God diffuses, as civilization creaks through time into Contemporary Myth and Polite Alibis of our Wretchedness, our Fear, by which I really speak our Corruption, shifts about the theatrical putty of its public fear and manipulates the levers of its Trick Language: the Priest whistles *Sin* through his nose, the Lawyer oozes *Crime* off his trick tongue, the Doctor barfs up *Disease* in a learned belch, and the Psychiatrist murmurs *Psychosis* through a sympathetic and enlightened yawn.

Sin-Crime-Disease-Psychosis . . . the shabby baubles of Corruption with which civilization excuses the murderous decay of Fear and Self-Hatred gnawing at its limbs.

Ah, but yet there is another of this ilk adept in the use of Trick Words and the vague secrets of manufactured knowledge; the Academician. Rather than particularize his humbug and limit himself to a single butchered portion of the body politic this Professional casts out misty nets of parasitical glab and pontificates upon "The Human Condition." One must never (even as a neophyte quivering in the lower echelons of the academy) expect a definition of the pompous platitude, but rather if one expects to get ahead in the Profession (ie: degrees, honors, tenure and the right, obscurely ordained, to becloud young minds and usurp the Natural Vision in preference for the Safe & Handy Formulas of a leechlike knowledge) one assumes (must assume!) the vacuous institution of "The Human Condition" and issue forth scholastic soap bubbles from the protective bathtub of official Education. The academician, like the Priest-Doctor-Lawyer-Psychiatrist, in order to stay in business, must insist that Man (the Poet . . . the Maker) does not mean just what he says, indeed does not really know what he means at all by the words he uses, that he really cannot understand his stance, his gesture, his own Illumination, his Sight, and that he, ahhh the hallowed Professional, must from his Uninvolved Structure of mathematical and clinical

reason and system interpret the Vision of Man for those
unfortunately unafflicted with Appreciation, must even
patiently elucidate to the poet himself what he is about
and insist upon formulized procedures in the commis-
sion of Vision . . . Iye! would even demand Perception
packaged into tight little syntactical games of polite
salability offered up in the Academic Economy as Unof-
fensive Amusements . . . Charming Things with which Effete Fellows and Vacant Ladies may massage themselves
without fear of actual arousement . . . geometrically and
grammarically pruned simperings of obtuse banality . . .
Perception clipped like a poodle without balls to pre-
clude the embarrassment of The Dog Show disrupted
by an Awkward Fuck . . . these Intellectual Transvestites
crouched in colleges and emasculating the Breath and
Sound of the Poet with rapid and bookish fingers in constant horror of thought of being spattered by the Jism and
Juices of Poet Song. (You will never NEVER find
either Kenneth Patchen or Henry Miller on a prescribed
reading list in any *required* college course in American
Literature). And these University Keepers of the Human
Vision smugly wonder with professorial indignation why
the Poets hate them . . . they who would make of Vision
a jingling pattern of cryptology . . . they who would stuff
Breath into measurable and precise diagrams . . . Profes-
sors of Literature/Tweedy Parasites crawling among the
Educated Acrobatics of Confusion . . . O Ye Hypocrites &

Knowing Ones rising in the secret of your own toilets to turn and view the vulgar turds thou hast left there hoping to induce an appropriate feeling of illness and disgust at the Internal movements of man . . . becoming all pissy and confused in the face of Voice & Vision like a Faulknerian maiden lady screaming "Rape!" before the Dark Intruder even unbuttons his fly.

Wait! I can feel my eyeballs straining to roll back up into my head and my tongue begin to slaver. Help Help SNAP! A hot hand's got me by the nuts! Allow me goddammit, allow me! A Poet is incapable of Lies! Don't feed me handy stuff! Don't tell me a bowler hat is boneless! I tell you all the civilized forces of purity have forced me to sign-up on the side of the Prurient Interest. That is to say, if an elephant were to piss through its nose at me would I move out of the way? I don't know. I just do not know. Do you see what I mean? I am very well aware that Noting Nothing Noddingly might just be cause enough to indict me on the seditious charge of Not Giving A Fuck, and I accept. Reasons? It's reasons you want? All right, you fuck'n snarf, listen: I climb on a streetcar and rattle down Market Street under a leering sign that shouts: Will Your Face Stand Close Inspection? For The Sake Of The One Who Sits Next To You GET RID OF THOSE PIMPLES! Now what kind of crap is that? I pick up the magazine section of a Sunday paper and am stabbed to the very bottoms of my eyeballs by an article titled: Can An Infected Tooth Cause Insanity? Here's another: this morning I read a news story about some nut who harnessed 2000 birds together, trying to make a flying machine from the fragile propulsion of birdpower. Here's another: I spot a cop standing in front of the City Hall and go over to him to ask what time the beatings take place . . . thaaawaap! . . . I'm just in time.

DO-YOU-SEE-WHAT-I-SEE? The bastards closing in from all sides. I can feel hate slithering beneath the vile carriage of time. I tell you it is only out of a sheer desperate defense that I affirm over and over again that my days are spent in the getting of love, idleness and drunk! Perhaps I speak thus because today I've been had by the spirit of Xmas and feel like I've been looted by a fag bandit. Exmass. Right! The getting of drunk. Get drunk enough and there's nothing in this rotting civilization of ours that cannot be made palatable by just another shot of juice. Moral Corruption when viewed through the skrim of lush becomes just another human eccentricity. If you drink enough, understanding comes easy. Great haystacks of sympathy clot me palping organ for that sad brother who got captured in the midst of those mad scribbling Brontë sisters full of their foggy fantasies and ruptured lust . . . vapors of their virginity leaking out the tips of their quills to clog the bogs. Oh me. Oh me oh no oh no oh me oh me oh me oh my.

Here now, I cannot let go yet. Stay on, STAY ON!

23.

"Why not, should be interesting to observe the techniques and sophistications of an upperclass fuck." Do I note a little sarcasm from that one? I can't bear a possessive Cunt, but my ego is flayed by an indifferent one. I am a masquerade . . . my emotions posture en costume . . . my passions parade in clever disguise and I bob about like a stark mime guessing which is which . . . here I peep behind a peacock feather fan . . . there I claw at a plaster cast of myself . . . I can't seem to find any player substantial enough to call Me—Myself—I! I see gesturing seductions from behind velvet draperies . . . I catch glances of Me again turning away in disgust at My vulgar motions . . . over there I catch the lisp of a simpering ghost . . . still farther down the lawn I sense the cautions of a heavy man trying to ignore the uncovered breasts of a lover . . . yonder hurries a taut scholar, his rare and airy brain seeping with sex . . . close under the streetlamp stands a thin young fellow in happy rags with foolishness curling his lips . . . and right here beside my victorious vision a young gent completely given over to the making of poems lies deep-pillowed down amongst his satyrist fantasies, his rapid fingers dancing along the crumbling edge of his private parts, wondering just how unmanly it would be to suck the perfection of his own cock, sadly rude at the thought that he has not the facile self-love of a narcissistic contortionist to tongue his own sex, his mind slowly becoming unglued until he must make do with a quick hand-job . . . (if you have illusions by all means harbor them; mine is not the purpose to spike the romantic in fevered imagingings . . . Glory Be & Piley Innards! . . . protect your ridiculous thoughts!) . . . ((against Me!)) . . . for a great pull downward has gripped my boots; that is to say, a gradual depression of personality. What? Well, my very good friend Mike Light defends against me as if I were actually crazy; he throws out Things for me to bobble with; i.e.: "I hear that you are mad at Kid Sorrow . . ." puff puff on a cigarette and an appraising glance at the ceiling while I am left to strangle on denials, gurgle and let words water out of my mouth like a tap being slowly closed off till only a hiss from the pressure is heard. Or else known fictions spun out by people whom I refuse to count among the living, but the cruel doubt of sly and gratuitous slander warps my righteousness more than if the lies were flashed in blinking bulbs across the side of the Times Building on New Year's Eve. The depression is as if two actual stones were sewn to my ears as I stared at the table dragging my head between my knees, my nose flattened on the boards. Come, here's another: One who lusts after my woman (this I know and we are both very polite in our calculations) sends me (and then quickly flies to a musical engagement in Cleveland) just a sneery clipping from out the newspaper that squarely rejoices at the supposed discomfort of a band of (be careful now) "Beatniks" . . . that's all . . . just that in an envelope with my name written upon it in green ink . . .

I show it to people (friends!) and am asked with a tolerant wave of the eye, "What's so horrible about that? Maybe he thought you would be interested." How can I cope with crap like that? I am so upset that a pimple has begun to appear about halfway down (or up, depending upon the respective states of my passivity or excitement) my cock . . . this has not happened since I was fifteen and could not keep hands off myself . . . it was the year I got my first lay, after which I swore never to do it again and would stick to masturbation as if my palm leaked moral glue. I lived within the confines of the sober dictum: A Cock In The Hand Is Worth Two In The Bush.

24.

An Upper Class Fuck Indeed! Dolly, as you can very plainly see, refuses to square with that hallowed old American saw: A fuck's a fuck. Hers is a social consciousness, and although she comes of rather slow-witted American proletarian stock, she is, by right of Natural Hungers and an honest and imaginative vagina, of the Sexual Aristocracy. I take my hat off to Dolly (or rather my pants, for she will fuck at the drop of a hat) and give out with a cheery Edwardian chuckle at the thought of comparison of my Dolly with the horsey female literati and intelligencia cooing over the ball-less young professor-poets who infect the Eastern academies for rich young snatches; fops more concerned with the Freudian improbabilities of lighthouses than the refreshing actuality of a good screw. Enough.

* * *

We gathered ourselves reasonably together and prepared to leave the automat, and during said preparations I observe Dolly stealing a memento of our visit to this vast departmentalized eatery . . . a few scattered pieces of silverware, the salt and pepper shakers and a small porcelain jar half-filled with congealed mustard. Undisciplined bitch! I crank my eyebrows at her but she pays me no mind, intent as she is in trying to stuff the chrome napkin dispenser into her coat pocket. I start to rise but am caught by the sight of Jarry absorbed in an intense study of the floor, or some unidentified object thereupon. "You ready to go?" I says a little edgy. Everyone seems to be getting hung-up in the preparations for leavetaking and consequently not taking any leave at all. "Wait a minute, man. Take a look at this," he answers, reaching down and picking a scrap of dirty yellow paper off the floor and handing it across to me. "What is it?" I says, full of suspects for trick happenings. "Read it," he says. I do:

"Daddy carrying Peter R.—Geo. Fox—& Booke
Rushes to candy drawer
Gets it out
Arranges plate (Mrs. H. not there beforehand)
Propositions the phantom on the wall
Gestures & Hands & Thumbs
Hurriedly eating—allows me 2 peanuts
Seems afraid to eat—I suggest it scares him—he nods
    drawing numbers in boxes & smudges them

I tell him he's worked a problem, "You've worked a
    problem."
(Elizabeth Willow is raising her skirt up to her chin)
He nods, "Yes, yes, and it's my problem."
I agree, defeated.
He messes a little (inside the lines) then he makes
    numbers more freely.
A dark one & a light one
Write it louder—write it softer
Then scrunching them all up
Then odd little symbols
Then much waving of arms of hands
& rushes back to the safety of numbers
There's a gay number
That one's feeling a little wild.
(not E. Willow this time but her friend Dirty Jean,
    dancing)
That one's almost out of hand
Then L. goes to time every number
good little neat little numbers
L. tries on my glasses
Then Humphrey tries to grope me
(g a s p !)
I cannot endure this and plead my eyes to The Gypsy
    Mother comes in, dripping ...f..

Jarry: Well, scoobeedoo, whither goes the goose?

Tully: Well, boy, I see it as the plot of a drama concerning the moonish machination of The Great Candy God.

Orick: It's to be expected, once The Fascist Plague gets its bleeding stumps in the door.

Dolly: Don't wave the Red Flag in here, you goddamn Deviationist!

Jarry: Here here, Pretty, none o'that Wobbly jass.

Orick: And may I ask just who is The Great Candy God?

Tully: The Galloping Anti-Christ, that's who.

Dolly: Horseshit!

Jarry: Not so vehement, Lovely, you'll split your taint.

Dolly: Piss on that taint! What does that taint mean to me?

Jarry: Everything.

Dolly: True . . .

Orick: He can't be!

Tully: But I tell you he is!

Orick: Can't be.

Tully: *Is*, goddamnit, *is!*

Orick: I'm afraid I can't swallow *that* flounder, Percy.

Tully: And *why* not?

Dolly: Yeah, why *not?*

Jarry: The upper ventricle in my pump is stuck. Me earlobes are filling up.

Orick: Here, let me give it a rap.

162

Tully: I repeat, *why not?*

Orick: Better?

Jarry: Much. Thank you, Pooh.

Orick: Anytime, Tim.

Jarry: You're much too good for this world.

Tully: I said, *why not?*

Dolly: Or the next.

Orick: You flatter me.

Tully: Did you hear me?

Dolly: Do we look deeef?

Jarry: Or dooomba?

Orick: Which reminds me, my belated old gray-haired muff of a mother used to have a tomb in her womb. My daddy told me so.

Tully: WHY NOT, GODDAMNIT, WHY NOT?

Orick: Why not indeed?

Dolly: Your father could probably tell you why not.

Tully: Fuck your father!

Orick: I resent that.

Dolly: If it's all the same, I do too. In-the-name-of-God-will-somebody-please-tell-me-why-not?

Orick: Why not what?

Tully: WHY NOT SWALLOW THAT FLOUNDER?

Orick: Which flounder are you speaking of?

Jarry: It would be more correct to say of which flounder are you speaking.

Orick: It is either correct or incorrect, it cannot be more

correct.

Jarry: I stand corrected.

Dolly: Personally, I brook no corrections. Of course, I can't speak for you.

Tully: I forget which flounder; you've confused me.

Jarry: Be gracious, Beauty.

Dolly: I try.

Jarry: We know that, Lovely, and we love you for it.

Dolly: And I you.

Orick: And I you too.

Jarry: And I all of you.

Tully: I've got it! I've got it!

Orick: Yes, what is it you've got there, Percy?

Tully: I've got The Great Candy God!

Orick: Who?

Dolly: Who?

Jarry: Yes, who who who? Pray tell us who?

Tully: Mike Light, that's who!

Orick: I'm afraid not.

Tully: Just what do you mean, *I'm afraid not?*

Orick: My dear boy, Mike Light is The Great Meat Scientist, *not* The Great Candy God.

Tully: HE . . . IS . . . NOT!

Dolly: See! You're wrong! Everybody knows you're wrong wrong wrong, but will you admit it? O no, not you, not old Bad-Headed McSwine! Never come right out and admit that you made a little mistake . . .

164

O no, not Tinsel Tongue Tully . . . not *him!* He just spins right along wrapping himself up in his idiotic mistakes, and if they'd let him he'd march right along in the Christmas Parade as rich as shit Shouting that Santa Claus was really Hitler. Wrong wrong wrong! Always wrong and never right, you crazy bastard! Everybody except you knows perfectly well that Aladdin Ginstrap is really The Great Candy God, just as everybody knows perfectly well that Mike Light is The Great Meat Scientist. Next you'll be going around saying that Paul Mistric is really Super Snarf and that Pantale Mantos is Frank Luke The Balloon Boy, and everyone will laugh at you because as always you are wrong wrong wrong!

Jarry: Give 'em hell!

Orick: Quite right, dear, quite right, except for one little point; Aladdin Ginstrap is not The Great Candy God . . . Garth Gobble is. Aladdin Ginstrap is Moon Mullins' manager.

Dolly: Suck a cock you sonovabitch!

Jarry: Give'm hell.

(. . . let it herein be expressed,
the author wishes to milk his distress . . .

s o b . . .! . . .)

25.

One might very well want to ask, "Who *is* this Jarry O'Rooney what gets the last word?" And I will tell you (very easily, could I not, if I were so whimmed). It is hard to tell you. It is impossible. If I had some paint pots and broken glass and some facile fingers I could paint his picture. If I had some rusty bedsprings and a Pisces Ladder on which to climb up and a double exposure of Artaud and a complete set of Excitements I could make a construction of his image. If I had a peeknuckle deck and a frizzled chart of the stars I could cast his fortune. I could even wheeze out a poem or two upon him if I had some old rubber type and a green candle. I do not. I cannot. I have not. I will not. Instead I will tell you around about him.

1. He travels in an intercontinental company of underground dandies, the membership of which consists of the following: Kid Sorrow, Billy Batman, George George

Bogardus, Philip de Fey, Mad Jack, Sigmund Marg, Young Peter O., Pantale Mantos, Paul Mistrie, Jesus Christ, The Man In The Bright Nightgown, The Leonic Ogre, Jack Snap, Aladdin Ginstrap, Fu Manchu, Sam The Turkey, Mike Light, The Great Snake Mother, John Garfield, Dolly Wobble, The Great Love Junky and (of course) yrs. trly., T. McSwine. The purpose and dedication of which crew is to observe the planet and all the Things thereupon.

2. He (Jarry O'Rooney) at about 2:30 P.M on November 18, 1959 in the city of New York said to me the following: "Ah cain't blow less'n ah'm blow'n wif Africans," by which he meant *real Africans*.

3. At approximately 9 P.M. on November 23, 1960 on 13th Street in the city of Portland he and The Leonic Ogre offered the circus presented in the following announcement:

Dr. Rooney Presents

Circus POETICUS MAGNETIQUO
Featuring: Clown Luna & Leo the Magic Lion & Troupe

GASSE GERMAN BAND
Vibrating Astrological DODO dome spectacle AT LAST!!!

GIANT FERN GODDESS ****** JASS
22 (count'em) jass bands

EARTH AYRE FIRE & h 2 oh
Magic Lantern Show

auction of lost OBJECTS

!!NAKED girls!!
balloons (baboons) flamingoes GIRLS a small rocket

THEATURE OF THE APOCALYPSE
5 (Five) Mythical Birds

THE AMAZING SYRINGE MAN

POEMS & WIG
Parasites & Drums Fireworks!!
8 Cosmo Mystique Apparati

mysterious ETHER ORACLE
&
WILD BEAST!

DOCTORS   Primitive Organs

TIMBRELS & PIGS

VEGETABLES & ZEPPELINS
(Christmas too)

COME COME COME COME COME COME
bang!

and 4.   A picture by Patchen (The Journal of Albion Moonlight): "A leaf falls to the ground. The eye of a rabbit has seen it. Make me such a design!" It is our own Jarry O'Rooney who is such a design.

26.

Orick, Jarry O'Rooney, Dolly and Me leave the Automat, suspect, under the stare of all the trick-talk'n hypes of Times Square and head for the hidden tubes. Down deep in the tiley grime of the frosty station we wait for the downtown local and watch an old Dip with palsied claws make a button-down no-shoulders type for about everything but his jockstrap. "Technique man, technique," Jarry whispers to me. I nod and the train shudders in leaking air.

Going downtown we sit silently reading dirty newspapers from under the seats. I lean back, contented with a hysterical copy of the Daily News and dig the chaos and panic that is breathing from the streets of New York, the lungs of the city breathing up murder, despair and the avarice of landlords.

We slither out into the air at 22nd St. and cross the street against the light as a fat cat in a blue cigar and a black buick bears down on us with horn a'blasting. Orick, skipping out of the way just in time to keep from being mashed into a glob, screams after him, "Missed me you greasy snarf!" Once across the street we pass a green newsstand with a big pencil sign, I AM BLIND, nailed to the counter. As we pass by Orick grabs a skin mag clipped to the overhanging top of the stall and moves on, scanning the beauties. We walk on, Jarry peering over Orick's shoulder, Dolly clanking beside me. "How come you are clanking?" I sez to her.

"It isn't me, it's the crap I boosted from the automat. Stuff is getting heavy."

"Get rid of it."

"Screw that, we can use it."

"Get rid of it. *I don't want my chick to clank.* People'll think I'm making it with a mechanical monster. Think I'm some kind of freak or something."

Dolly stops, walks back to the newsstand and dumps the silverware onto the counter. She looks at me. "The rest of it," I say. She lays down the salt and pepper shakers. "The rest of it, goddamn it!"

"Aww, Tully, I want to keep the other thing."

"Out!"

"Geezus," she mutters as she wrestles the napkin holder out of her pocket and clunks it down. The blind geezer inside is starting to freak out, not knowing what is going down, and is calling out in a terrified voice, "Who is it? What do you want? I'm blind. So is my wife. Don't hit

KIRBY DOYLE

me!"

"Take it easy, pal," Dolly says. "Here's a present for you." And pushes the stuff across to him. "Here you go," she says as we walk on, leaving him pleading, "Please . . . please . . . I have no money . . . don't hit me . . . I'm blind . . . so is my wife."

Jarry and Orick are standing under a streetlamp arguing like fury as Dolly and I walk up to them. Each has a grip on the skin mag with one hand and points furiously at a page with the other.

"I tell you it's shaved!" Jarry shouts.

"Goddamnit, and I tell you it isn't!!" Orick shouts back.

"It is, it is!" Jarry shouts back.

"What's the hassle?" Dolly asks.

"I told this idiot that I couldn't bear it when they airbrushed the cunt away in these skin mags, and he said it wasn't airbrushed, only shaved and her cunt was too far under to see the slit. What kind of crap is that, I ask you? Makes me wonder if this infant has ever seen a twat at all. Ha!" Orick says with magnificent disdain.

"Spy the Spastic Snatch!" I shouts.

"Shut up Tully!" Dolly said without looking at me. "Let me see the goddamn thing!" she said, grabbing it out of their hands. She squinted at the area in dispute. "Sorry baby," she said to Jarry, "but it does look like an airbrush job. From this angle you'd see some split if it were only

172

shaved, this way it looks as is she hasn't got any cunt at all and judging from the caliber of this near pornography, that seems improbable."

The young lady in question leered from the page with a bogus seductiveness that suggested success in at least one aspect of the movie industry.

27.

Miss Kids lived in a wandering loft that extended through the entire third floor of an old and seemingly abandoned nut and bolt factory on 6th Avenue. She lived there, between periodic fits of shrill melancholia followed by a dank nunlike chaste reclusion during which all communication with the outer world would be squeezed down to a terse note to the grocer to leave her grub at the bottom of the stairs. Secluded she might stay for weeks, the ending to which seclusion would be a general announcement of an impending bacchanal in her rooms with all invited who wished to come. Her given name was some preposterous monicker like Phyllis Benbow Beardsly, but she was called Miss Kids from her habit of addressing each and everyone she knew or didn't know with a shrieking, "Kids! Hello hello! Yes yes, it's terrible! I'm dying, you know, quite dying, my dear Kids!" or some variant upon the general theme of her psychic or sexual condition, but always with the salutation of "Kids!"

As she got to know you and through repetition remember your name she would amend it to "Tully Kids!" or "Michael Kids!" or "Teddy Kids!" or whoever you happened to be. The same went for whatever she might be discussing. If it were politics she might screech out with, "Oh, Ike Kids is just a sex-starved old woman!" or "I think Fidel Kids is just *too* clubby!"—an uncertainty existing in her speech as to whether the ". . . Kids . . ." was placed, thus, "Fidel Kids . . ." or thus, "Fidel, kids . . ."

She was tall, close to thirty years of age, had a very long, thin and, consequently, rather beautiful face, a rather awkward body made more so by her jerky gestures, and what could only be called "tan" hair that fell in wisps across her eyes that probably had something to do with the constant flutter of her hand about her face. She kept what she liked to think of as a secret list of her ex-lovers that she sadly enjoyed showing only to people with whom she stoutly refused (I suspect out of fear of making her come) to go to bed with, like me. The list numbered about twenty-five of the top money-making names in American Arts & Letters. I never failed to feel a shudder of jealousy (or perhaps envy) whenever she insisted upon showing it to me. This because, I suspect, I was, in a sort of crackpot manner, in love with her. Perhaps "in love" is a bit strong, but I had *something* working . . . (vague stirrings . . . slight floweration of the penicular gland . . . the beginnings of a bulge below my belt . . . and then . . .

BANG! . . . a full-blown hard-on!). The Leonic Ogre has indicated similar feelings, also a little tale of maddening quality: Me and Kids was down in this gin-mill one night, see, and we is getting terrible oiled and I am scheming how to get her in the fart-sack without a big hassle and a lot of scream'n, when right'a the clear bluey night she turns to me and hollers, "O Leo, Leo! Take me home and fuck me, fuck me, fuck me!" Well now, Tully boy, I liked to shit right in me shoes. Before she can shriek another obscenity I ups, slams her in a cab, and in ten minutes I got her in the bed and I'm fumbling at me fly. Wop! into the feathers I dive and grabs her by the snatch, but instead of throw'n her legs up over me ears she lets out a whoop, leaps from the bed and stands there howl'n, "What are you *doing* in my bed? Don't point that nasty thing at me! Get out! Get out! I thought you were my friend, Leo . . . I didn't think *you* would try to take advantage of me! Get out! I'll scream rape! Get out!" There I sits astounded, getting terrible pissed-off and losing my hard-on. "Shut up that scream'n, you silly bitch," I yells, "or I'll punch you in the fuck'n head!"

"Get out! Get out!" she lets out with again.

"Get out, hell! You're the one what said 'take me home and fuck me,' and that's what I'm trying to do if you'll shut up that scream'n and get back in bed." But it was no go, Tully. It was just like she reached down and snapped a padlock on her snatch. Wasn't nothing to be done but roll over and go to sleep. Goddamn silly bitch!

And so thus, Kids.

28.

The party was boiling when we arrived, strange-looking people bulging from the windows. Miss Kids was standing at the very top of a skinny flight of stairs, screaming at her guests. As we start up she looks down and screams at us. "Kids! Make yourself welcome!"

"Cut the crap, Kids!" Dolly shouts back as we trudge up the stairs.

"Thank you for the kindness, dear," Miss Kids replied vaguely.

"O, Tully Kids, so nice of you to come. You must have heard about the free booze. Come in, come in."

"Hi Kids, how's the lock on the old chastity belt holding . . . Dr. Freud been able to pick it yet?" Orick asked gaily.

"Yes, yes, you worm, so good of you all to come," Kids said, smiling blankly and beginning to ignore us as other people crowded up the stairs. We moved off into the general direction of the hootch, scenting our way through myriad folks, all talk'n some shit to each other and lushing it up. As we moved into the jabbering crowd Jarry leaned up close to my ear and whispered, "The joint's full of Warlocks and wizards, man. I can't stand it!" and as I looked around he disappeared into a dusty puff. It's all coming together, I thought, and battered my way onward.

I found the kitchen, wherein I found a long resplendent table, whereupon I found the juice, a jug of which I stashed under my coat, and with Dolly in tow (Orick having been sucked into witty repartee with a very sexy young bit of upper-crust bohemia) headed for a little out-of-the-way stop uncluttered by human types to explore the visionary possibilities of what looked like a rather expensive make of bourbon whiskey. In one of a series of white-washed rooms an obstacle in the form of a tangled bunch of very clean people politely arguing presented a blockade to my single-minded passage. With one hand on the bottle and the other gripping Dolly by the wrist, I edged into the group and was just about to burst through when a smart-ass type who looked like he might correct grammar down at PMLA, grabbed my arm (the one with the bottle under it and I began to panic) and tilting his head back so's the end of his nose was on a level with his eyes, sez to me with the words come'n out his nose, "And what do *you* believe in, my good fellow?" and his eyes snickered back to his skinny friends.

"Why ah believe in just about everything."

"Like what?" he snorts.

"Well, like you and me and the jam jar, Jim. Scuuuuse me," I sez and oozed through the mechanical silence left in the wake of my smiley journey. No straw-men now, Tully, I tells myself. They're too inflammable and a spark out'a yo brain is liable to set 'em afire and burn down de pad. Be cool.

Plop Plop. All over the place I hear well-rehearsed ideas dropping like buttered stones.

Not being able to find an uncluttered corner in which to sit and nip, I pull Dolly down onto a vacated cushion against a wall and prepare to dig the goings-on down among the shoelaces and cuffless britches. We sit and sip, passing comments back and forth upon the oily mechanics of social recognition. "Don't look now, Tully, but you're being fucked from afar," Dolly whispers. I look anyway, feeling sort of flattered, and catch a well-anthologized fag poet with thin hair spying me. Howdee do, I nods, and he blinks back from behind his tortoise shell spectacles like an oldish sewer rat caught gobbling a turd. He comes snaking over to me with his hand fluttering like a skin flag. "Tully McSwine, where *have* you been hiding?"

"In the movies, man, in the movies."

"Really?" he sez, swallowing some spit. "How charming," still holding onto my hand like it was really my cock. "I've been *expecting* something from you for quite a while now."

"Yeah? Ya have huh?" I sez, trying to remove my claw that was getting all sweaty from being held, but he wouldn't let go.

"Oh yes, and let me say that I thought your long Motorcycle Poem in the issue of 'Zounds' was simply beautiful," and gives me a little squeeze.

"Ya did, huh?"

"Quite beautiful, yes, quite. Are you working on anything now?"

"Oh yeah."

"Another long poem?"

"Naw."

"Oh, prose?"

"Uh ugh . . . self preservation."

"OK, sexy, if you can find a free hand how about pass'n the juice?" Dolly sez, look'n at my left ear. I do.

"Oh, yes, I see . . ." he says, looking over his shoulder for an opening in the crowd.

"How about you . . . you working on anything?" I reply somewhat presumptuously, seeing as how he's been one of *the-promising-young-poets* for at least fifteen years.

"Well ah . . . why yes, ah . . . I'm putting together a book of my ah, letters, ah . . . in a book, ah . . . yes . . . the Pennycracker Press . . . it's, ah, called 'Epistles', ah . . ."

"Crazy, ah," I says.

"Yes . . . 'Epistles' . . . charming . . . your poem . . . really

. . . I mean . . . quite beautiful . . ." his head clicking back and forth over his shoulders like a wind-up toy gone gaa gaa. "Oh, there's Aladdin! I really must go say hello to him. I'm off!" he fluttered, then turning to me as he dissolved into the gay mad party-goers, he cheeped, "And I'll see you later. Ta-ta!"

"Over my dead snatch you will!" Dolly shouts after him.

"Crazy, ah," I says smiling at the spot of vacant air he left.

Dolly and me sat on the cushion, leaned up against the wall, slugged the piss out of the juice, and watched all the campy little chirping groups press up against each other like they was copping a mass free feel. The whole pad was packed with thirtyish type artistic folk dressed in sloppy good taste. There was a gang of seedy young poets and painters with their straggly molls sullenly eyeing the rabble, probably figuring the best defense is a glaring silence. And actors too, all blanky good-looking with their hair artfully tumbling about their brows while they unembarrassedly bandied about the most banal garbage with egocentric intensity. Glab glab glab glab, everyone vomiting in everyone else's ear. A sturdy looking little group with guitars and faded blue-jeans and a sort of leftist militancy came marching in. Reed College political types; the girls all very homely and intellectually agressive in a vacuum-packed sort of way; the college boys all lean and bushy and intolerant. All of them a bunch of sexual cripples, which they will sternly prove by fucking at the drop of a political sympathy. Oceans of come would flow tonight, I thought as they began strumming some hackneyed chords out of the guitars and burst into song with 'We Shall Not Be Moved.' I figured it was time to take a leak.

"Got to relieve myself, dear Doll," I said as I rose from the cushion and eased the bottle from her hot little hands. "Be back in a minute. Don't get lost or gang-banged."

"Don't worry about me," she smiled sweetly. "Just put that thing back in your pants when it stops leaking." Vulgar bitch!

Pheew! You can never really tell how stoned you are until you rise to yer feet. I wheeled around the room a few times trying to find the can and finally grabbed a haughty looking type in tweeds, pipe and blond handle-bar moustache, by the arm so that he jerked to a halt and the booze from the glass he held slopped all over his french-cuffs. "Say pal, where's the crapper?"

"I *say!*" he said, glaring at me. "Y've made me spill'ut!"

"Sorry, buddy," I says, trying to sop up the booze with my own coat sleeve, "but I got to piss so bad my teeth'er float'n. Where's the crapper?"

"I assure you, I *really* wouldn't know!" he said, drawing back.

"Then what the fuck good are ya?" I shouts at him. He

moved off cautiously, keeping an eye on me till he was swallowed in the crowd. In the next room I spots a door with "JOHN" printed on it in big pencil letters. I ups to it and grabs the knob to go in. "Just a minute there, young man, it's being occupied!" I looks around and spots this withered-up little turd in a shiny suit and pink fingers with the nails chewed down. He had the stench of a book-reviewer about him and for a moment I thought of piss-ing all over him. "What'a ya mean 'it's occupied'? How many's in there, a dozen?"

"Ina Reddley Hensen is using it at the moment, and so if you would just kindly wait I'm sure she'll be finished . . . ahh, that is, out very shortly," he squeaked through his little mousey mouth and folded his hands on his belly as if the last word had been said.

"Ina Reddley who?" I says.

"Ina Reddley Hensen," he answers very neat like. I stare at him hard with my best hoodlum look and he begins gulping. "Miss Henson is the foremost Middle English scholar in the United States," he said uncomfortably.

"And you're waiting here for her to finish taking a crap?"

"Well, I . . . well really!"

"That's OK, don't apologize . . . I'll use the sink," and I slipped through the door to come face to face with Ina Reddley Hensen straining to loosen the gluey shit from her bowels. I must have caught her with a turd half-out

184

because she gave a little jump off the toilet seat like her asshole had severed the turd in the middle and the last half had gone shooting back up into her rectum. "That's alright, stay where you are," I murmured pleasantly, "I'll just use the sink and be gone in a second. No trouble at all, I assure you. I'll turn my back and you can pretend I'm not here. OK?" I said as I hung my joint over the cold edge of the porcelain. I looked up into the mirror over the sink and saw her sitting there with her mouth open and her arms held out straight in front of her like she was trying to repel the barbarian invaders single-handed. I smiled politely in the mirror, then remembering her specialty I decided to put her at ease with a little something familiar. "Summer is icumen in: Lhude sing cuccu!" I sang out with and flashed her a big friendly grin. The strike of horror across her face vanished and, sitting straight up from the crouch she was in, she bellowed back, "Groweth sed, and bloweth med, And springth the wude nu. Sing cuccu!"

"Bravo!" I clapped. "Bravo!"

"Yes, yes, it's one of my favorites. It's such a gentle little thing."

"Oh yes, yes, one of mine too!" I beamed. "Do you know the thing Mr. Pound did from it? 'Winter is icumen in: Lhude sing Goddamn!'"

I rolls back me eyes. "Raineth drop and staineth slop, and how the wind doth ramm!"

"Sing: Goddamn!"

"Wonderful!, you're in good voice," I said, stuffing my cock back into my pants.

"Oh, do you really think so?"

"Beautiful, just beautiful."

"Thank you, thank you. One doesn't get the chance very often."

"How true."

"It does one good to give out song every now and again, don't you think?"

"Like a lark in a meadow with the sunshine bubbling down on ya."

"Oh, how pretty. Are you a poet?"

"No, not a poet. A vagabond. I have sold myself into vagabondage, not poetics."

"And is it a hard indenture?"

"Next to poetics it is the breath of simplicity itself. Absolutely no devices to be maintained, no trick languages to be manipulated, no attacks of hysteria to be defended against. All that is needed is a sturdy pair of eyes and a strong grip on the gonads of fright."

"Then you are a seer?"

"Nay, I told you . . . a vagabond."

"But you search."

"Not even that . . . I only look."

". . . and see . . . ?"

". . . nothing . . ."

"Nothing?"

"Nothing."

"But if you look, how is it that you see nothing?"

"Madame, I peer and peer thru the sunny cellophane of my soul but sight nothing."

"Seeing, you see nothing?"

"*Looking*, I see nothing."

"But how is that?"

"I cannot see because I have no Sight, therefore I have no Vision. A Seer is a Visionary, and so knows what is Sighted. I do not. It is this that makes me less than a poet."

"But you look."

"Yea, and in Looking I become more than just a cabbage-seller. It is because I look but do not see that I am inferior to the poet, but it is because I look at all that I become superior to the sellers of cabbage. I stand between the sightless citizen who knows nothing and the Vision of the Poet who Knows all. One is a stillborn whose corpse is manipulated by the civilized machinery of death, the other cannot die. Either stance fills me with horror. I stand between them, rejecting neither though one cannot live while the other can do nothing but. I envy neither. I interpret one to the other. I urge the dead to look at the living, and the living to look at the dead. Each can learn much from the other, each is part of The Plague and would, if it had the means, destroy the other. The Poet hates the citizen with as much vehemence as the citizen hates the poet. The poet writes with a murderous intent as intense as the social castigation used by the citizen, but the poet attempts to destroy with weapons that have no effect on the dead, as the weapons of the citizens have no effect on the poet. One uses life against death, the other simply reverses the formula, so rather than victory or defeat there is merely stalemate. The threat of poverty to the poet is as ridiculous as the threat of emotional lobotomy is to the citizen. When, if ever, these threats are switched, then, and only then, is there a real danger of the spilling of real blood by, between and from both poet and cabbage-seller. To each the other is a very dispensible commodity, the absence of which would make this world a much nicer place. The citizen sees the poet as a shit-disturber bent upon disrupting the quietus of death, while the poet sees the citizen as a grasping vegetable intent upon the incorporation of death. Each will and does rape, burn, maim, murder and destroy for the preservation of his stance. It is difficult for me to keep from loading the gun in favor of the poet, but I think of the tyranny of poets terrorizing even each other with the awful calculation of their Vision as imprisoning as the intolerance of citizens. I am neither cabbage-seller nor poet. I am a vagabond because unlike the poet I cannot See, but rather only Look, and unlike the citizen I cannot accept a daily issuance of death. How awful it is to be forever dead, and how equally awful it is to be unable to die! I, vagabond, stand between them, a minute-by-minute continuum of life, a second-by-second encroachment upon death. I have not a single answer for a single question. A bit ago some cultural fop asked what I believed in and I could not answer, I could only mutter that I believe in everything, and that is not an answer, it is a statement of existence. I literally believe in everything. It is all here and you can make none of it go away. If there is a prime difference between myself and both the poet and the citizen, it is that they believe they can make it go away; I do not. The poet thinks he can make it go away because he thinks he can make it better than it is; the citizen thinks *he* can make it go away because he thinks he can kill it. The poet thinks he can better the planet because he understands it. The citizen thinks he can kill the planet because he does not understand it. They are both nuts. It cannot be changed, it cannot be killed; it can only be walked upon. Anything else is a fiction designed and used as a spiritual message by those who think this globe is here to be used as a cork to stop up the leakage of their own manufactured inadequacies. I neither demand mighty efforts of production from myself nor reject that which I do produce, I merely go out and walk upon the planet and look at the things scattered thereon. I look, and I like and I dislike, but I change nothing, nothing changes. I *cannot* change anything. The fact that nothing changes is not at all distressing; this, because everything is different, nothing is the same, and so one cannot become bored with the static quality of each thing, for there are so many things, all different, at which to look. I cannot spend time on trying to change something, either bettering it or killing it, because if I do so I will miss the other things while my attention gets all mossy in its concentration. You, Miss Hensen, are a Chaucerian scholar . . . unfortunate. I say unfortunate because while neither Citizen Chaucer, Clerk of the King's Works, nor Poet Chaucer, Chivalric Visionary & Questioner, nor Scholar (forever a curious cross and conflict of aspirations poetic *and* prosaic) Chacuer, Inditer of Astrolaboic Treatise, would look askance at your studies, Geoffrey Chaucer, Pilgrim-Vagabond, would think it strange that you should worry your brain so upon his gentle journey in which he only watched the human movement across the globe. *That* was important to Chaucer, so important that its beauty could not escape the immediacy of his pen as could and did the concerns of Citizen, Poet and Scholar Chaucer. As Pilgrim-Vagabond he invented nothing, improved nothing, killed nothing. As Pilgrim-Vagabond he only recognized. As Pilgrim-Vagabond he was only concerned with looking at that which is before the eyes, which is everything; and when his eyes screwed down to analysis and became beady on one object to the exclusion of the planet, then he becomes uninteresting and carpy. Shakespeare speaks to the planet, and is therefore great. I do not care for the dry prettiness of Bloomsbury-type writers any more than I care for the hero-bully type of cowards who have strangled American writing with terse lies these past thirty-five years, yet I believe it was Forester . . . I think it was, who said: 'An examination paper could not be set on the Ancient Mariner as it speaks to the heart of the reader, and it was to speak to the heart that it was written, and otherwise it would not have been written. Questions only occur when we cease to realize what it was about and become inquisitive and methodical.' Do you see what I say? To me, wisdom is instantaneous and intuitive. I am not at all sure of what I know, less so of what I Understand, but if I Know or Understand anything it is this: it is all here; it will not go away; I do not want it to."

At the conclusion of my speech Miss Hensen was fiddling with a roll of green toilet paper and showed signs that she was desirous of wiping her ass but was reluctant to do so in my presence, and so displaying that discretion for which I am known and loved, with a courtly little bow, eased myself backwards out the door and right into the arms of a terrible ruffian-looking chap. "Here now, I got'cha!" he growls.

"Far be it for me to argue the point," sez I, "but I should like to inquire into why you are attempting to wrench me arm from me shoulder?" All the while, as this muscular bounder was tussling me about, the little old guy who I had encountered upon first entering the john was dancing around us crying, "That's him, that's him alright! What did you do to her you . . . you . . . pervert!"

"Yeah, you pervert! what'a you doing to her in there?" the big guy grunts and twists my arm up to the back of my head.

"Pervert! Pervert!" I shouts. "Why you bunch of bubble bite'n snarfs, thats a fight'n word! Call me a pervert and I'll cut ya up and put ya in m'gravy!" with which I tears one hand free and, plunging it into my pocket, I comes out a'flash'n with my six inch spring blade. "Call me a pervert will ya, cocksuckers!" and with the big fuck still holding one arm I twists about and takes a slash at him neatly severing his necktie three inches below the knot. "Here, here, what *is* all this commotion?" Miss Hensen fortunately was arriving through the door of the crapper.

"These two pee-hole bandits called me a pervert and were trying to assassinate me!"

"What ever in the world for?" says sweet Miss Hensen.

"Are you alright, Ina?" the little guy peeps.

"Perfectly. I've never been more so in my life! What *are* you and Mr. Buncher doing to Mr. . . . ah . . ."

"McSwine," I offered.

". . . Mr. McSwine? Mr. Buncher, do leave go of Mr. McSwine, and Mr. McSwine do put up that horrid knife, and do stand still! Thank you. There now. Now Mr. Crawly, will you please explain this outrage upon my very dear friend, Mr. McSwine?"

"But Ina, Miss Hensen, this *person* broke into the . . . ah . . . while you were, ah . . . occupying, ah . . . it . . . and I naturally thought that he had, ah . . . well . . . assaulted, ah . . . you."

"Do you mean rape? Oh my dear Mr. Crawly, how very generous of you, but I'm afraid McSwine here was entertaining no such intentions. His purpose was merely to relieve himself in a urinatory fashion, not a seminal one."

"But I told him that you . . . well . . . that is, he should have waited!"

"Not at all, dear fellow. Have you never felt the immediate summons of nature and must need answer it without delay or face an embarrassingly damp consequence? No, no, Mr. McSwine was quite right in his actions. There has been no harm done, no dignity shattered, no unpleasantness produced other than what you brought on. Quite the contrary, for Mr. McSwine and I had quite an interesting, I would even say inspiring, chat. Mr. McSwine and I both fully understand the mechanics of the eliminal process and feel no embarrassment or disgust for that which simply is. You, Mr. Crawly, I fear have been terribly frightened by civilization. You should pay closer attention to your Chaucer." Then, turning to me, she smiled graciously and said, "Mr. McSwine, let me present your misguided antagonists. Mr. Crawly is the Chairman of the Department of Humanities at the University at which

I reside, and Mr. Buncher, besides his studies in that department, is also the star fillback on the football team."

"Fullback," Mr. Buncher corrected.

"Fillback, fullback . . . is there a difference?"

"Why sure, there ain't no fillback in football. The fullback is . . ."

"Shut up, Buncher!" Mr. Crawly hissed. Buncher looked unhappy.

"I must be off, Miss Hensen. I am awaited by a lovely lady who, I fear, will be captured by a wandering lecher if I prolong my absence. Goodbye, my very dear Miss Hensen, and thank you for the wonderful chat. I've not had such a good time since dear dead Grandma used to puke on the linoleum and let us kids skate in it. Thanks again and goodbye," I said, folding back into the gathered crowd and waving.

"Goodbye, goodbye, O noble Mr. McSwine! I wish you happiness on your journey! Goodbye, goodbye, till we meet again!"

"If not in this world then in the next!" I called out, now completely out of sight.

When I struggled back to Dolly I found her surrounded by an odd assortment of brilliant young horny types. Harold Bulwar, a great shaggy boy-giant who wrote secret and turgid prose-poems upon the silence of the moon and other unintelligible subjects, was standing beside her, hanging his head hot with shame at the richness of his dirty thoughts. Mike Light was there too; he, the militantly uncorrupt, who marched his manhood off daily to combat the trick wars waged by the national hysteria of competitive intellectuals; he who must suffer through his third and last incarnation under the pain of his own human fallibility. Beside Harold and Mike there was some goggle-eyed young idiot who, as he carried on in queezy English, seemed to be trying to rub up against Dolly.

"You do that again, you son of a bitch, and I'll kick you in the head!" Dolly was saying.

"But you are slave. I do anything to my slaves," he said.

"How would you like to take a flying fuck at a rolling donut?" she says.

"You detest me," he says.

"Fuck'n right I do!" Dolly answers with a steely eye.

"Everyone detest me."

"I shouldn't wonder."

"All the enemies detest me."

"Congratulations."

"I have no friend, only enemy and slave."

"You rub that greasy body up against me again and you won't have to worry about no friends or enemies."

"I do care not eef you detest me. Everyone detest me. My slaves detest me. My Mother detest me. My Mother ees a dog."

"Yeah? Do you detest her?"

"Yes. She try to punish me, but I weel not let her. She ees mad."

"Why does she want to punish you? I could understand it if she wanted to kill you, what mother wouldn't, but why only punish?"

"I tell you she ees mad, and religious. She ties me to bed and try to deflower me but I treek her and weel not let my sex get hard. She thinks I have not slaves. She know I beat my slaves and make them sex before me. She know that I am pure and must stay virgin and so she try to deflower me. Eef you were my slave I would make you do sex before me. I would call een all my slaves and make them do sex on you and I would watch and masturbate."

"Masturbate?"

"Yes, I masturbate every day. Eef I do not masturbate, my juice weel sour een me and make me urge to do sex. I am virgin. Eef I am not virgin my slaves would run away and my enemies would keel me. I masturbate every day to keep my juices pure. I masturbate and make my slaves catch eet een leetle vials and when I capture enemy I make heem drink one of the vials and then make him become slave. My mother would like to capture my juice. She ees enemy. Soon I will make her slave."

"You come on like a terrible drag, man."

"What ees 'drag'? Ees it intelligent? I am intelligent. My slaves tell me that I am intelligent."

"They been lying to you."

"I masturbate."

"Yeah, yeah, OK, you masturbate. Big deal."

"I masturbate every day. Eef I am eating meal at night and remember that I have not masturbate I will stop my eating and masturbate then."

"You need a good piece of ass."

"No no no no no no no! I weel not sex! My fingers! My fingers! My pure fingers do me! Do you have whip?"

"Nope, no whip."

"I am intelligent."

"Horseshit!"

"I am beautiful. You desire to sex weeth me."

"O, my god!"

"Geev me your hand. I want to suck your blood."

"You do and you'll end up on your ass."

"You detest me."

"Vehemently."

"Henry Miller ees enemy. He ees vulgar."

"Who is this asshole?" I says to Mike Light.

"Some trick Spaniard name of Christobal. Seems he's got the Ford Foundation snowed into thinking he's brilliant. His con is talking the same trick shit over and over again. He went through the same act about an hour ago and had a bunch of fruity foundation people all creaming their pants. I think he writes plays, or pretends he does." Hearing his name mentioned, Christobal turned his baby face toward me, bugged out his goggle-eyes, and set his rubber lips to working. "Do you theenk I am beautiful?" he says to me.

"FUCK NO I don't think you're beautiful!" I says back at him.

"You are an enemy."

"Fuck'n right I am."

"I weel make you slave."

"Piss on you."

"I would like that."

"Stick around, it might be arranged," I say pleasantly. His eyes get a little steamy and he turns to Dolly. "Ees he your lover?" he asks.

"That's him, indestructible Tully McSwine!" she beams.

"Do you sex weeth heem ?"

"Do you mean fuck him?"

"Do not say that! Eet ees vulgar and impure!"

"You're a real asshole, Jack."

"Ees hees sex large?"

"Tully," she says to me, "why don't you dump this prick on his ass?"

"He's more your size."

"Why don't we sell him?" Mike politely offered.

"Sell him?" I says.

"Sure."

"Who to? Who in the fuck would give good money for *him*?" Christobal was digging what was going down and wasn't too happy about it.

"Bellevue. They pay fifty bucks a head for certifiable psychotics. We could say he attacked us."

"It's pretty obvious he's a bona fide nut . . . there wouldn't be any problem in getting him certified if we just drag him down there and let him babble to a head-shrinker. Do they give you the money on delivery or do we have to wait?"

"Cash on the barrel-head. We split it right down the middle."

"We better tie him up. You got a rope?"

"I'll ask Miss Kids. She ought to have something lay-ing around. Keep him here, I'll be right back." Mike split in search of Miss Kids and Christobal began flicking his goggle-eyes back and forth between me, Dolly and Har-old as we began closing in.

"Where did heem go?" he croaked a little hysterically.

"To get a rope. He'll be right back. Be cool. Here, have a drink?" I says holding the bottle out to him.

"No drink! I weel no drink! Why heem go for a rope?"

"Take it easy now. No one's going to hurt you, we just going to tie you up, that's all."

"Weeth a rope? You tie me weeth a rope?"

"You catch on quick," said Dolly.

"Cool it, my love. We don't want to excite him," I says soothingly.

"Here Chris, have a snort. Sit down and tell us about yourself while we're wait'n for Mike to get back with the rope. Now what was this you were saying about slaves?"

"No slaves! I have no slaves!" He looked nervous enough to shit a blue marble.

"Well now, Sport, I hate to call you a liar but I did hear you say you had all kinds of slaves." And I looks to Dolly and Harold for confirmation. They both nod sagely.

"Heard him myself with my own ears," Harold said. "Said he had a whole passle o'em."

"That's right!" Dolly chimes in. "Says he makes 'em do all kinds of dirty things in front of him. Filthy, disgusting things!"

"I have not dirty slaves! You are crazy! Ha ha!" A little panic from that one as his baby fingers make rapid motions with his buttons.

"Makes 'em jack him off into little bottles," Harold smiles.

"I do not care about you!" Christobal shouts and looks around for an opening in the crowd.

"And makes other folks drink it. Nasty!" from Dolly.

"Not drink! Not drink! My fingers!"

"Hang'ns too good for 'im."

"Ought to make him drink his own little bottles."

"Cool it," I says again. "Lets not get him too shook, we haven't got him tied up yet."

"I go now!" he says, and makes to walk off.

"Just a minute there, Sport," Harold murmers and grabs him by the shirt front. "Mike'll be back in a sec' and then we'll go take a little trip 'cross town."

"I take no treep! I go now!"

"Now just hold on a bit and everything'll be jake. We're go'n to see some nice folks that'll treat ya good . . . lots to eat and a warm flop. You'll like it there."

"No treep! I must the Ford Foundation! Ha ha! I go now!"

"Ha ha yourself, you goddamn pervert! You ain't go'n nowhere!" says Dolly.

"Not pervert! Fingers!"

"And little bottles full of come . . . yeah, I know. Now just hold still till Mike gets back with the rope."

"I do not like rope! Ford Foundation! I not care about you. I am intelligent! Ha ha!"

"Shut up or I'll rap ya in the head!" Dolly hold'n up a fist.

"Fingers!"

"Here comes Mike!" I shouts, having spotted Mike struggling through the crowd and waving a clothesline over his head.

"I cannot rope! I have not slaves! Only fingers! Ford Foundation! I have not leetle bottles! I am friend! Ha ha! Goodbye!" and he gives a violent jerk, leaving Harold holding a fistful of torn shirt-front and leaps into the crowd.

"He got away!"

"Head him off Mike, he's coming your way!"

KIRBY DOYLE

"Spread out!"

"Herd him toward the back of the house!"

"Where'd he go?"

"That way! Toward the door!"

"Do you see him?"

"No! he's too short!"

"Fan out like they do in war movies!"

"He's hiding down among the shoes!"

"Is he armed?"

"Only with fingers!"

"All-thee-all-thee-oxen-free! You can come out now, Christobal!"

The four of us ran through the crowd shouting directions to each other, but Christobal eluded us in the pack of bodies and we ended up in the far side of the room flushed and panting and a little drunker from the chase.

"Aw fuck it!" Harold puffed. "I'm pooped. To hell with him."

"Fifty bucks shot right in the ass," says Dolly.

"He's probably safely in the bosom of the Ford Foundation by now," I said and took a snort out of the bottle I still clutched in my hot hand. "Let's find a quiet corner to do up the rest of this juice and lament our loss."

"Thanks, but not me," said Mike Light. "I gotta go home. I'm expecting a reply from the new president on a matter of great concern."

"Yeah? What dealings have you got with our national heroes?"

"It's a matter of seeing justice done to the Birdman of Alcatraz."

"Who?"

"The Birdman of Alcatraz. I sent the president a letter on his behalf. I said, 'Release Robert Stroud or I will kill you.' Doesn't sound too pushy, does it?"

"Oh, not at all, not at all."

"Good! Well, I'm off. I'll let you know if I get any action."

"Yeah, yeah Mike, do that. See ya." He split and I began to get uneasy and bugged by the clatter of the crowd, the clank of a couple hundred tongues.

"Let's find us someplace quiet so's we can drink," I said.

"I don't wanna drink, I wanna dance." Dolly being impossible.

"Dance, schmance. Let's drink."

"I wanna dance!"

"OK, you dance, Harold'n me'll drink. Come on Harold."

"OK, go lush it up, but I got my eyes on ya. Don't fuck up!" Dolly said, shaking her tongue at me.

"Wouldn't dream of it my love. Come Harold." With Harold behind me I set off to find a subdued spot in which to get peaceably oiled. Shouldering our way through the crowd, we started trying doors, but in each of the rooms a number of people were either screwing or trying to and I had no eyes to get spattered with flying come or curly hairs. We worked our way clean through the pad without finding an empty room and finally ended up in a pitch black little passage that was so narrow my shoulders scraped the walls as I moved through it. I lit a match and we followed the passageway around two or three tight corners to where it suddenly ended smack up against a tiny green painted door with a great big bronze padlock hanging on it. "Where'n the hell does that lead to?" I said.

"Damned if I know," Harold replied.

"It's locked."

"Yeah," said Harold, wrapping his fingers around the lock and slowly pulling the hasp off the door.

"Very neat," I complimented him and entered. I lit another match and spottted an old-type lamp with a stained glass shade that had a glass bead fringe dangling from it. I snapped on the light and looked around. The room was a large one with the walls painted a dull fuchsia. A huge, pure white fur rug completely covered the floor and smack in the middle of it stood a gigantic carved oak swan bed with a deep velvet blue covering. Swollen pastel pillows were scattered all about the room, some of them big enough and soft enough to sleep on. All the walls were covered and dripping with huge oil paintings, watercolors, drawings and photographs of Miss Kids standing, sitting, lying down, smiling, frowning, dancing, sleeping, crying and even fucking (6 black and white, 3 in color, 1 watercolor, and a whole series of very intricate pen-and-ink things). In each corner of the room a huge moist and waxy jungle plant was creeping up to the ceiling and extending tendrils around and across the paintings to completely obscure some and add new dimensions to others. Scattered about the edge of the room were six or seven spidery little tables and stands with long thin and carved legs delicately holding the weight of hundreds of unrelated objects, statues, small gold boxes, ornate bottles, fans, toys, old cracked and splintered books, keys, candles, beads, jade ashtrays, cigarette holders, gilt mirrors. Hundreds of little unidentifiable gadgets teetered silently in the lushness of the room.

"It looks like we come across her inner sanctum." I said. "Here, have a drink. Rejoice!" Harold ups the bottle and downs a mouthful without letting tear one leak from his eye. He handed back the bottle and began walking slowly around the room picking up objects in his big hands to examine them closely and then replacing them exactly where he found them, very meticulous like.

"Well, Hal me son, this here looks to be some sort of paradise where she formulates her fantasies and flattering fictions." He said nothing but looked at me like there was a stone growing out the side of my head and kept moving quietly around the room. Glug glug I take a long draught from the jug again and my thoughts begin to take on the texture of oatmeal. I stumble over to the big swan bed and let myself silently gravitate down onto its velvet covering. I look around but it becomes more difficult to focus on any part of this room stuffed with her mementos.

"Ha ha, I know what it is!" I shout. "Her sexual magic manufactured here in the secret opulent rooms of her alterexistence. Imagine, if you can, and mind me, dear Hal, I'm not questioning your imagination, imagine, I say, the misty doings that go on here. Enchantments spun out . . . charms wafted over the city . . . conjured images . . . rites . . . hexes . . . imagistic fixations . . . somnambulistic voodoo . . . juju to dream upon . . . weird life-sized spiritual fucks . . . pronged by pulsating poltergeists . . . the seduction of magic dolls . . . *had* by the spirit world. *Are you listening, Harold?*" He stopped wandering for a moment and turned to me.

"I'm listening."

"Good. Now have a drink." I tossed the near-empty bottle to him. He neatly picked it out of the air with one huge blond paw and tipped it up. "Good," he said.

"Fuck'n right it's good. Any left?" he held it up in the dim light, gauging the level. "Yeah, there's a little left," he said and flipped it back at me. I gasped down one good swallow and held the bottle up neck-down over my head. "Cooo," sez I. "That was some pretty good drink'n whiskey while she lasted." I lay me head down on the big goose-down pillow and the old bed started a'rocking.

"Pheewwweee! I done it again . . . got my head all turned around . . . think I got my ass on backwards. Goddamnit, Harold, hold still there! Stop rock'n the goddamn boat . . . ye'll fling me in the sea!"

"Lay down, Tully, you're drunk."

"Yer rooty-toot-toot-right I am! Very observant lad you are. Deserve a prize. Come'ere an' ah'll piss in yer pocket."

"Later," he said and turned back to the room.

"Later, schmater! You know better than that. You're drunker than I am or you wouldn't say that. Later! Horseshit, later! If there is any trouble at all with this buggered world, and mind you I'm not saying there is . . . NOT SAYING THERE IS ANY TROUBLE WITH THIS GODDAMN WORLD AT ALL . . . *are you listening?* . . . have you heard a word I've said . . . rap once for yes and twice for no . . . I said if there is any trouble with this globe of ours at all it is because of this *later* business . . . insufferable . . . *intolerable!* . . . not later but RIGHT NOW . . . I mean fer Chriiisake look around you, Harold! I mean . . . shit! . . . the thickness of blindness *is here in this room!* . . . Take that white desk . . . *are you drunk again?* Poor lush bloated boy, can I help you? Perhaps hold yer boozy blond head while you take a puke at the world?

"PAY ATTENTION!"

207

I said, take this white desk a'clattering with bronze ladybells, rusty atomizers, jap matches, a ceramic kif pipe, swans and blue bottles shouting flowers . . . *are you hearing me? My warbly message? Want me to turn up the volume so's I come in better? Listen, you bastard you, you better not frink-out on me!* . . . I said look there on that white desk! Seven leapers! Headless pencils and italic pens! A satin pro-kit with beads! An old Negro ear! A four-pronged Chinese bamboo snatch scratcher! A thin volume of delicate pornography! Two squeezed tubes of KY jelly! Four eucalyptus leaves! Red paper birds! Letters from Kid Sorrow! Old jewels too, it seems . . . everything is there, nothing left out . . . later, gone, nothing missing! all the pigs' bones of her crumbling past . . . the whole Tattooed Countess bit . . . I mean I love this girl, in a rather archaic fashion . . . want to lay her that is . . . Geezus love ya, Harold! Little Geezus love ya! Was it you who shit three times in her bathtub, leaving three neat little piles of offal so even-spaced? How gay and mad yer drunken bowels must have danced . . . and she and poor Pip coming home in the dawn wanting to bathe and play . . . look where yer scatalogical orgy has led: then gentle Pip (Ahab's darling? "O Captain, my Captain, come back!") now a poet in a madhouse ("Hands off that holiness!") . . . she, fluttering in Asia . . . *git yer fingers away from that dial you goddamn secret snarf, you can't turn Me off!* . . . I said take this wall a'dripping with eleven genuine handpainted pictures of her all staring at the bed quaint where she hid her sex in a bush of short gilted hair. Tell me, Harold, how many times do you think she has bounced off these walls? No, goddamnit, don't stop now to count the public dead. Answer my questions!

Did I tell you that she was scared of my black leather soul? My bloody boots? My dirty hair? ME?

I kissed her once you know. She slid her tongue down my throat like a meal of fresh oyster . . . distressing! Here now, wait! Let me sob. Let me blow my nose.

Here now, look around this room . . . everything top-heavy with a teetering morality . . . a douched passion smelling of pepsin . . . all desire bundled up like in the pre-Raphaelite lushness of an old dentist's office.

Listen Harold . . . what? You have to puke? Then use a dresser drawer . . . or a wastepaper basket . . . leave something behind.

Listen, wonder if one early morning (a hollow bottle sweet singing sickly) at the very end of a valo colored rainbow, that white desk there began to speak . . . a voice bathed with hysteria crashing up from among the chalky fingers of her stale fantasies . . . button bone and a torn bedsheet . . . in fact, Harold, a goddamn ghost low moan'n with a burning snatch . . . that voice! "O, Kids, whatever am I going to do? I can feel it lurking right there inside me! *That Man's Hand! In My Womb! Opening and clos-*

ing like a hot feathered FIST!" . . . What then, huh, Harold? Eh? Goddamn it! Zap! What then? Gaaaaaaa! Listen! A Golden Foot is stomping on her head! Her Iron Wings dragging in the dust! Hot Damn! Whips! Sweet suffering icicles of piss frozen from her window-sill! Her Hidden Orgasm discovered! Deceived! Defeated! A Black Tongue Licking Smoky Messages from a'twinkst her candy coated thighs! The Erupting Eye of an Old Poet's Tool? ARE YOU LISTENING? Ha ha, you bastard! *Let it happen!* Shake for a prelubricated Crucifixion! Incestual Fingers reach past her nailed feet! Woof Woof! Yeaaah! Spikes! Instant Explosions of Sex & Doom copulating like Bright Beasts on the obscene merry-go-ground of her mind! Icons breathing lashes of Destroyed Passion upon the secret nudity of her hot dirty bedroom! A slow Worm travels the passages of her body! Between her toes! In her armpits! Eyebrows! Lips! Sex constricts! Glistens! Painted Fairies dip their toes in Her Blood like amused ladies trailing lace in a Hanged Man's Come! Coward hands grip her breasts and throw soiled milk like a Midnight Whale EXTINGUISHING THE SKY! Listen you, goddamn you, Harold, you listen! Hear it! Chanting . . . effete poltroons chanting from behind the spiked windows of a poem . . . "Cheat The Worm & Burn The Corpse!" (I burst into applause . . .)

29.

Night fits. Drink softens the pain barrier and I sink down into contemplative yet abject melancholia. Clunk. Clunk. Clank. The organs must suffer but I, ahhh yes, but I feel no pain. Ding-dong dong-ding ding-dong and dong again, my dears. Dolly as always must struggle me and place my weapons beyond reach. It is her robust penalty and punishment.

30.

I try to keep from making demands upon myself but it is useless. I command myself to stop, and myself refuses. Do not lean upon yourself, Tully, do not lean so hard, but it does no good. My bowels grind out their chore twice daily; my tongue leaks saliva upon the instant of foody smells; my cock swells to erection like a fleshy mold at the merest flicker of a sexual nuance; the jungle rot between the 4th and 5th toes of my right foot bubbles with delight-ful agony demanding a good five minute rubbing that will leave it throbbing and cracked; the tiny piles that ring my ass hurt almost deliciously behind the press of my finger until they too ache and my sphincter seems ready to drop out; I blow a bit of blood from my nose each dawn as I batter myself up out of sleep; there are times after sex that I am locked out of my body and must bang on my eyes to be let back in, and then, once in, feel like a thief in a dying house; I see a cat's silhouette in my window; dusty crones howl the stairs; a Western Union boy lost is rattling my

windows, five raggedy scarves envelop his ghostly head
... watch! ... the stairs have teeth ... the doors close in
the gloomy dawn ... his fingers wander my windows ...
he suffers my name ... I read the mistaken music and
confuse the bleak with the mysterious ... my heart sweats
... the landlord listens and lies abed with eyes a'swelling
... I think in the dark of the streets filled with cripples
and the days of indecision through which I worry, stealing pink lightbulbs from Woolworths in the afternoon,
leaving myself notes of cynical instruction at night to be
discovered in the horrible morning: "Only do fun things
..." ... visits to the library, where I set my mind wandering onto former conquests and ultimate defeats ... Dolly
loves me very much, but I do nothing ... I think my wrist
is broken and that the break is slyly moving toward my
neck ... we go to Central Park and The Museum of Natural History and as usual I am a bastard, and there are so
many people watching ... I lure myself into unhappiness
... I close my eyes tight and see only gaudy patterns and
mutations of light ... tighter and I become completely
limited by my own geometry ... I open them and the
ceiling becomes banal ... I close them again and am now
trapped by a large peeling sign reading, 'Dixie Peach Hair
Grease' ... I switch on a light and brace myself to read
... I pick on Prescott and open to find, "The sacrificial
stones of the Aztecs were convex ..."; I do not think I can
take this crap much longer, and if not they shall all read:

"He shot out his life with a gunne!" . . . which is to say, he
went to sleep . . . and he dreamed:

It was in this dream that in the summer we all (all the
g h o s t s !) went Sunday sailing up Bad Richard's Slough
on the good John Good and down she went! Good God
Jesus Jimmy, women, children, strong men and picnic
baskets, shouting, screaming, waving arms and hankies,
everything going asshole over rowboats, the pond afloat
with flame'n debris. I dive, holding my waving organs
against the impact. The captain (our beloved skipper) up
to his hard beard in the murky blue giving orders (an inner calmness rampages). Old types panic into the arms of
a well-deserved death. Sigmund Marg (my Weird) stands
on the far shore shouting vile oaths until a hot cinder gets
him and he goes poof into a hungry red ash. Kid Sorrow (knee-deep in the gore of his past habits) grapples
with The Man In The Bright Nightgown back and forth
across the rotty fore'peak (anchor chains flapping in the
smelly air) like some darkly spooky types excercising in
the hateful day. Mad Jack sits cross-legged astride a glowing windlass and surveys the whole scene with a wasted
indulgence (while really nervously a'flutter in his pocket
the remnants of a tattered roach burns on). I have a swollen urge to speak out against such an inhuman day but my
tongue melts in my mouth. O what a crummy conflagra-
tion! Such fiery doings! I sink! I float! I sink again! There
are other folks doing the same. On the bottom I rejoice

. . . there is nowhere to go but up. Everything seems like a bad looking-glass. All is seaweed and bellybuttons. Before my watered eyes passes a vision of my best boyhood friend playing it fast and loose with my pet collie. Revenge!! I am maddened! I feel a revolution boiling in my hair. The fat bottom of the John Good comes settling freely down through the above watery wastes over my head. A dinky little kid is in the way . . . The Call To Action! Am I the man my father was? Air bubbles leak from my ears . . . the baby is DOOMED! . . . tough luck, Tim . . . I know only the law of the jungle . . . up I float . . . I am struck with the bends . . . nitrogen bubbles in my nose . . . I break the surface like a whale . . . goose-colored daylight seeks me . . . I come up in the midst of a floating patch of pre-diluvial flowers covering the surface . . . Help Me! . . . flappy arms . . . Help! . . . Help! . . . strong man rowing . . . I am *saved!* I am covered with sheets of sunshine . . . I am pulled aboard the lifeboat gingerly because I am covered with oily mung like in an old war movie . . . First Aid is rushed to my side from Mexico . . . I inhale deeply while Mad Jack slyly searches his breast pocket and pretends.

ABOUT THE AUTHOR

Kirby Doyle was born in San Francisco on November 27, 1932. In the contributor's bio that he provided for the Spring, 1958 *Chicago Review*, he summed up his early life: "Was a juvenile delinquent for the first 16 years. Am well acquainted with the insides of various police stations and other minor prisons. At the age of 16 I left home to join the army, see the world and find out about life. I saw the world and found out life wasn't real. At age 20 I returned from finding out about life and went into (1) marriage (two children), (2) poetry, (3) and the scholarly life. Am now 25, a graduate student at San Francisco State College, and an Associate Editor of *Transfer*."

After leaving the Army, Doyle enrolled in culinary classes at San Francisco City College but later transferred to San Francisco State College to study art. It was there that he attended lectures and readings at the school's Poetry Center, and enrolled in a class taught by Kenneth Rexroth, considered the "founding father" of the

San Francisco Renaissance of American poetry. Early poems by Doyle were published in *Transfer*, the San Francisco State College literary magazine; poet/painter Wallace Berman's *Semina* magazine; John Wieners' *Measure*; and Michael McClure's *Ark II/Moby I*.

Doyle's poems appeared alongside works by Jack Kerouac, Lawrence Ferlinghetti, and Allen Ginsberg in the Spring, 1958 issue of *Chicago Review: Ten San Francisco Poets*. He was also included in *The New American Poetry: 1945–1960*, Donald Allen's highly influential anthology of Beat Generation and post-war poetry. Doyle's first book, *Sapphobones*, a collection of 36 short lyric poems written between 1957 and 1959, was published in 1966 by Diane di Prima's The Poets Press. Also, in the mid-1960s, several of his poems were published by The Communication Company, the publishing arm of the Diggers, a radical community-action group of activists, artists, and actors based in San Francisco's Haight-Ashbury neighborhood.

According to Doyle, *Happiness Bastard*, his only published novel, was "written on a sojourn that my lover post-wife and I took to New York in 1959–1960." Similar to Jack Kerouac's *On the Road*, the novel was composed on a single scroll formed from taped-together sheets of paper. Writer, editor, and publisher Raymond Foye described it as "a brutal work of black humor born of Doyle's own struggle with poverty, drug addiction, and unhappy love affairs" and "one of the great lost novels of the Beat

Generation." The novel was submitted to, and rejected by, several publishers before it was finally released in 1968 by Essex House in North Hollywood, California. Essex House was a short-lived publisher of primarily soft-core pornographic novels, although, in their defense, they also published three original Philip José Farmer sci-fi/fantasy novels as well as Charles Bukowski's *Notes of a Dirty Old Man*.

Struggling with drug and alcohol addiction, Doyle stopped writing shortly after the publication of *Happiness Bastard*. In his autobiography *Sleeping Where I Fall*, actor Peter Coyote, a central figure in the Digger community, recalled Doyle's lost years: "He had just published his novel . . . and although not yet certifiable, he was working toward his credential, shooting speed and spending his nights discoursing in erudite, epic rambles. . . . Kirby went to pieces and disappeared for a time." Doyle spent several years living in relative seclusion in small towns and communes in the Mount Tamalpais area, approximately 50 miles northwest of San Francisco.

Tisa Walden, friend and publisher of Doyle, wrote that after this period, "Kirby collected himself (self-corrected like a gyroscope will)." He returned to San Francisco and, in 1983, had his first major collection, 200 pages of poems, published by Greenlight Press, which was run by Kaye McDonough, poet and former wife of Gregory Corso. This was followed by three chapbooks published by

Walden's Deep Forest Press, and another chapbook published by Ferlinghetti's City Lights. During this period, Doyle also composed the epic poem *Pre American Ode* and a novella, *White Flesh*, both still unpublished.

He remained a mainstay of San Francisco's North Beach literary scene until a lengthy hospitalization for dementia and diabetes, eventually passing away on April 5, 2003. A memorial poetry reading was held for Doyle the following month at the New College of California. The poet Michael McClure said of him, "He was a handsome, big-smiled Irish American rascal. He was an original Beat, loose-jointed, with a great laugh. His poetry was beautiful stuff."

ACKNOWLEDGMENTS

Profound thanks are extended to the following for their generous financial support which helped to defray some of this book's production costs:

Stephanie A., Kevin Adams, Hussein Al-Momen, Mohammad AlRashed, Rune Andersen, Adrian Astur Alvarez, Zeshan Askari, Jeff Atkins, E.R. Auld, Robby Bailey, Thomas Young Barmore Jr, Chris Beat, Steven Belletto, Cameron Bennett, Dudgrick Bevins, Brad Bigelow (NeglectedBooks.com), Matthew Boe, Brian R. Boisvert, Dy Booth, Giacomo Boschelle, David Brownless, Daniel Buckle, Jason S. Buhrmester, Chris Call, Shane Calvert, ZiG Chad, Scott Chidister, Wesley Chien, Jerry Cimino, Chelsea Clifton, C. Colla, Jangus C. Cooper, Mike Corkery, Sheri Costa, James Costello, Parker & Malcolm Curtis, Travis DeSilva, Dylan & Sam Doomwar, David Edmonds, Curtis B. Edmundson, Isaac Ehrlich, Lars Staffan Engström, H.F.S. Evans, Rodney David Falberg, Pops Feibel, John Feins, Dennis Forsgren, Nathan "N.R." Gaddis, Jaak Geerts, GMarkC, Damian Gordon, Kelly Graham, Christopher L. Grassi, Mark Allen Gray, Adam Greenfield, Richard L. Haas III, Elizabeth O. Hackler, Frank Hagen, Erik Hemming, Aric Herzog, Isaac Hoff, Jonathan Hope, Reuben Huntley, Neil Glenn Jacobson, Brian Jagodzinski, Billy Jarvis, William Jewett, Jakob Inooraq Johannesen, Erik T Johnson, Kristiana

Josifi, Haya .K., Gautham Kalva, Crazy John Kerecz, kkurman, Kurt Johann Klemm, Dr. Tracy A Knight, Elif Kolcuoğlu, Dan E Kool, M.D. Kuehn, Paul Kuliev, Izzy Ladinsky, Mark Lamb, Jean-Jacques Larrea, George P. Lauber, Lew Lewis, Marilyn Jaye Lewis, George H. Lieber, Gardner Linn, Sheri Lynne, Louis M-N, Brian de León Macchiarelli, Sharn Matusek, James May, Jim McElroy, Peter McGee, Donald McGowan, Sean Brendan McGrath, mdtommyd, Jack Mearns, Sergio Mendez-Torres, Tim Mentuis, Tim Merrill, Dr. Melvin "Steve" Mesophagus, William Messing, Jason Miller, Spencer F Montgomery, Steven Moore, Brian A Morton, Geoffrey Moses, Gregory Moses, Annie Ngo, Rick Ohnemus, Michael O'Shaughnessy, Daniel Pack, Danny Paige, Kelly E. Pavlik, Derek Patton Pearcy, Andrew Pearson, Amy Pettinella, Ry Pickard, K. L. Pinkoski, Poems-For-All, Stephen Press, Waylon M. Prince, Patrick M Regner, Benjamin Riddle, Judith Ringle, Rob, Kayla M. Rohde, George Salis, Frank V. Saltarelli, Christopher Sartisohn, Kurt Schreiber, Steve Seward, Jake Silver, Kenn Sisson, Brian K Skillin, Christopher Slajus, Jason Smith, Justin M Smith, Sid Sondergard, Giuseppe Spice, Martin E Stein & Scott A Saxon, K. L. Stokes, Elisa Townshend, Cato Vandrare, Laki Vazakas, Rachel Wells, Christopher Wheeling, Isaiah Whisner, Karl Wieser, Charlie C. Wilcox, Charles Wilkins, Matt Williams, Jeff Wilson, Carl Wiseman, Morgan Witkowski, T.R. Wolfe, Bob Woolley, Serena Zaccagnini, and Anonymous